Sunsets & Margaritas

Christine Lynn Lourenco

BookLocker
Saint Petersburg, Florida

Print ISBN: 978-1-64719-513-7
Epub ISBN: 978-1-64719-514-4
Mobi ISBN: 978-1-64719-515-1

Published by BookLocker.com, Inc., St. Petersburg, Florida.

Printed on acid-free paper.

BookLocker.com, Inc.
2021

First Edition

Dedication

To my father, Edward Leppin, who was always my biggest supporter, I love you and will miss you forever.

Chapter 1
The Event Biz

The music vibrated the windows outside the nightclub where the red carpet was lined up with photographers whose flashes blinded me. A lot of young Hollywood talent was here including a mix of reality stars, and single actors and actresses from television and movies. I was supposed to be here to work this event, or so I thought. Instead though, I was walking the red carpet, and everyone was taking my picture. Blending in was not something that I could ever do in this town, but that was all I wanted to do. When I finally made it past the sea of media, I entered the club to the sounds of cocktails being poured, loud music and dancing. It was the grand opening of the trendiest club in Los Angeles. The club was absolutely stunning and in the hippest, coolest part of Los Angeles but I felt so done with this scene. They shelled out big bucks to get the popular stars here and make it at least seem like this was **the** place to be. We had set up a VIP room inside for celebrities who had come to mingle away from the masses. My employer hadn't even really assigned me to do anything at the event except to go to the VIP room and talk to celebrities and make them feel welcome. I really think that having me work here for them, actually was simply good publicity for them. I wanted to do more. I was here to learn, and do something to make a difference but was never given the opportunity. I was so frustrated in this job. It felt meaningless.

After graduating college, I got this job in event planning and was actually excited to do something on my own instead of doing what was expected from Hollywood – following in my father's footsteps. As you can imagine, living in California in the Los Angeles area, there are tons of opportunities to run events. There isn't a night of the week something isn't happening around here. It could be a movie premiere, a new boutique opening, a nightclub celebrating a reality star's birthday, or a group of bloggers hosting vendors for a feature. Los Angeles was a mecca for events. My social calendar could be permanently booked, and I could make a living just showing up at parties and being paid to be there if I wanted to. After all, this is celebrity central and I should know. I grew up in this Hollywood lifestyle and was the daughter of the most famous actor in the world. I didn't even really have to interview, and I would get a job. Anyone would die to hire Alexandria Thompson. I have never done one bit of acting, yet I often found myself in magazines and gossip columns. I never even really went out socially and kept to myself. I studied hard when I was young, stayed out of trouble and got a college education. I graduated magna cum laude and started working as a Manager of Event Planning. The problem is that everywhere I go in this town, everyone knows who I am for the most part. So, even once I graduated and now had this job, everyone at work made it seems like I could do no wrong just because of my name. I knew it wasn't authentic. I could not show up at work for two weeks if I felt like it and still have my job (but of course I didn't do that). There are so many people with bad intentions, and I never knew who really liked me for me.

This latest event that my company was handling was a new exclusive nightclub opening and we had invited celebrity guests to help kick off the opening night and give the club the image of exclusivity it desired. While the event was fun, it further yielded the celebrity existence that I didn't want to be a part of. Plus it didn't help that I was putting myself out in the public more and more each time I participated in these events. Photographers took my photos just as much as any celebrity endorsing an event. I was just as famous. This job was exactly what I didn't want and although I should have never took it, I don't think I would've realized it until I experienced it. It didn't take long before I woke up one day and recognized that I couldn't do this anymore. I knew that there was so much more I could offer to a company but more importantly, I needed to stop selling myself short. I could contribute to society in a much better way than this. I called out sick the next day to give myself a long weekend. I just needed to focus on some self-discovery. And, the latest issue of People Magazine showcasing images of myself mingling with the rich and famous, was the icing on the cake of giving me a stomach ache. The images suggested these were my friends and my lifestyle, yet most of these pictures are situations I was forced into because of my job and not where I really wanted to be. It was all a show, a façade and a circus wrapped into one.

What did I really want? For one thing, I didn't want to be running events that cushioned the already fat wallets of the rich and famous. What purpose did I even serve? My whole life I was soul searching. I had everything people would die to have but there was always something missing. People always look at the rich and famous as not being human. We were considered privileged and untouchable but in reality, we are simply flesh and bones and the same as anyone else. I knew one thing for sure, and that was that I wanted to give back. My whole life I had been given so much and there were so many families who had so little. I wanted to make a difference and taking this job was not something that made me feel pride in myself. It just drove me further and further into the self-indulgent lifestyle of this world. I would be headed down the same path and have the same ego as my father. My father didn't ever have to lift a finger. He had staff to do everything for him. Sometimes I would even have to go through one of his assistants just to reach him on the phone.

I shut the door of my bedroom after calling out sick on a hot Friday at the end of July, pulled out my laptop and started exploring other jobs across the country. I have always been so conservative but for the first time, I think in my heart I knew I had to do something risky and extreme to change my circumstances. Before I started my job search, I couldn't help but see the news that was trending on my computer's home page. There was the nightclub opening from the other night, and although the nightclub grand opening has nothing to do with me, the local news covering it uses my photo when talking about it. Most people I guess would be happy to have this coverage, but I didn't want the attention. Fame was not something I wanted to explore as I had seen what it did to people firsthand. The foremost thing I needed to do was to get out of this town. I needed to go somewhere where I could just be myself, where hopefully I wasn't recognized, and I could be treated as an equal. I didn't need to be on the pedestal that so many people placed me on. I just wanted a job where I could have fun, do something I love and make a difference. And most importantly, I wanted people to get to know the real me without knowing my background.

But where would I go? I didn't want to go to New York City or Miami because I knew people would still recognize me, although not as much as Los Angeles. But, I also knew I would need to live and work somewhere at least near a major city so that events and event companies were more abundant. I thought about New Jersey quite a bit. My mind kept going back there even after searching other places like Portland, Chicago and Dallas. New Jersey seemed right for some reason. It was located next to New York City but more low-key. Growing up, we stayed there often. My father had owned several homes through the years on the famous Jersey Shore. I had always been an avid surfer and most of our homes were on the coast. I knew New Jersey well and if I could help it, I wanted to live by the ocean. New Jersey was actually pretty similar to California except for the weather. There were beaches and mountains, farms and vineyards. I felt comfortable there, and I wanted to finally be on my own and feel what it would be like to stand on my own two feet and not in the shadow of fame. We still had property there, but I wanted something of my own. I wanted a fresh start.

I started researching non-profits but wasn't having much success and most event companies were in New York City. Finally I found one company that was event based but all of their events and activities had a charitable focus or gave proceeds back to the community. This was EXACTLY what I was looking for. Working somewhere doing something I love but being able to give back to others. I was tired of egos and self-indulgence. I would rather boost the confidence of an amazing person making a difference or help out a family that is struggling. There is so much more to life than money. Helping others, living your life with kindness and being passionate about following your dreams is what described me. This company seemed like the perfect fit. It was near the coast, not too far from New York City, and had the type of event management I was looking for. I anxiously looked on their career tab of their web site and noticed straightaway they had a position open. I immediately submitted my resume and crossed my fingers. I used my father's New Jersey address on my resume so that it wouldn't discourage them from looking at me. I didn't want them to know I lived in California, at least not until they saw me in person for an interview. My current company did events mainly in Los Angeles but we had things in New York and Miami too that we covered so for all they knew, I lived locally managing those events closer to this market. Plus, they were a small firm and probably didn't have the budget to relocate someone for this role. All I could do is hope they would call! I looked up the company on LinkedIn as well and tried sending some notes to network with individuals who already worked there so that I wouldn't get looked over.

This was only my first step to making a change but already I felt different. Instead of doing what was easy and expected, I was doing something I really wanted even if the road to get there wasn't so easy. I didn't want to be handed this job like I had been handed everything in life. It would be meaningful to me if I got this on my own just for my background and skills, and not my last name. I needed to figure out what was important to me and who I was as a person. Deep down, I knew that I wanted to give back to less fortunate people. For some reason, it was just who I was. I was ready to make that dream a reality and this small company in New Jersey could be just the ticket to get me there. I just had to hope and pray they would call me. This wasn't Los Angeles, and I could just tell an acquaintance that I like this brand, and they would offer me a job. But, if I got this role, it was because "I" got the role, not Alexandria Thompson, daughter of Alexander Thompson – the famous actor.

It was a Friday, so it was a good day to have called out sick with no events this weekend for once. The house was quiet and my father was away so there were no helicopters or drones flying over trying to get that golden picture. It was about 3:00 p.m. when I headed down my driveway, and the guard opened the gate and I got out of the house to get out for a bit. I was in a good mood and excited by the secret adventure to a new me. Plus, my drive would bring me to see one of my closest and true friends. I was going to meet up with my friend Claire, who I had met in college, for drinks and appetizers. We had been wanting to catch up on life and I had a lot to tell her, even it was still all just a dream. We were meeting at a place in LA called the Broken Shaker. It was a hip bar located by a rooftop pool so the vibe was fun and relaxed, but we loved this place because it had the coolest, hand-crafted cocktails we had found in LA. As I pulled up to valet my car, my cell phone rang and I figured it was Claire making sure I was here. She hated waiting at these places by herself. But to my surprise, I didn't recognize the number and when I answered, it was about my resume…already! I tried to contain my excitement and keep my composure. I immediately had chills running down my spine, and my hands felt clammy and nervous grasping the phone.

"*Hi, is this Alexandria Thompson?*" asked a woman on the other end. "*Yes, this is Alexandria. Can I ask who is calling?*" I inquired. "*This is Jordie from Shore Events. We received your resume and would love to have you come in next week for an interview. Would you be available Monday or Tuesday at 8:30 a.m.?*" I tried to contain my eagerness as I responded "*Thank you so much Jordie. Monday at 8:30 a.m. works, and I am very excited to meet you and the team.*" The woman told me she would e-mail me the street address and interview details as we hung up the phone. I couldn't believe it! My hands were shaking as the valet drove away with my car leaving me standing there. I felt nervous, happy and lucky just to have gotten this call, and couldn't believe how quickly they had responded. Maybe this was really meant to be? Then it also hit me as I realized I was sitting in Los Angeles and had to make it over to New Jersey this weekend to be there for this interview on Monday, but I didn't care. I didn't have the job yet, but I couldn't help but be enthusiastic. Now, I really did have something to share with Claire!

I took the elevator up to the rooftop feeling like I was floating in a dream and with a huge smile on my face while texting Claire that I was on my way. I was still smiling ear to ear as I hugged Claire and said hello. She could immediately tell that I was up to something and asked me if I had met someone special. I just laughed at her, and we ordered some guacamole and chips and two of the tastiest cocktails we could find on the menu. Claire was not involved in the celebrity world at all growing up, although she was of course surrounded by it living in this area and now had some celebrity clients in her line of work. Claire had grown up in San Francisco, California. Her dad worked in the technology sector and her mom was a nurse. Claire went to college with me, and we had roomed together. My talented friend is now a fashion stylist and is working for a boutique at the Beverly Center. She was living over in Beverly Grove, a convenient community near the Beverly Center. What I had always loved about Claire is that she is down to earth and creative. She knew the real me too. I knew I could always trust her, and she had become one of my closest girlfriends. She knew about all of the contacts I could provide her but she never once asked me for help.

"*So, loop me in on the event world. I saw all of the pictures on social media of all the celebrities at your latest venture but I can't help but feel there is more to your smile. Did you meet a guy?*" inquired Claire with a grin. I laughed as I sipped my cocktail and responded "*No, I did not meet a guy but yes, it's been a whirlwind at my job but I am* ***not*** *loving it at all.*" I rolled my eyes and took a big sip of my cocktail and then continued. "*And, yes, I do have more going on that is contributing to my smile. You are not even going to believe this and maybe it won't even go anywhere, but you know how I had always mentioned to you that I grew up going to soup kitchens, volunteering at dog shelters and doing anonymous acts of kindness and how much I enjoyed it?*" Claire knew me inside and out and her proud smile reminded me of that as she urged me to continue. "*Well, I found this company in New Jersey that is also in event management, but they have a charitable twist to each event. They give back to their communities or causes but the best part is they are interested in interviewing ME on Monday!*" Claire gave me a quick hug. She knew how important this was to me, despite the fact that I could very easily just not even work at all and lounge in a pool all day if I wanted to. "*That's amazing Lex! I would hate to see you move across the country but I understand why it makes sense for someone like you. And, the company sounds right up your alley for sure.*" I couldn't agree more.

Claire and I finished our cocktails while fending off the advances of annoying men and laughing about our crazy college adventures. Claire was someone I knew who liked me for simply being me. She knew the good, the bad and the ugly about my life. She never questioned anything and just accepted me. She also never asked me for anything. So many people have tried to get close to me in order to meet my father as a way into the acting world. I knew I had found a true friend in Claire, and I was lucky to have her. She knew me as the girl with no makeup, wearing my college sweatshirt and sleeping till noon when we didn't have class. We were just two girls experiencing college and being on our own for the first time. We had grown up from kids to adults together. I would miss her terribly, but I also knew I could come back and forth as often as I wanted. That was the one thing money could buy me – being in important people's lives no matter where I was.

I went home later that evening and booked a flight for the following day to Newark, New Jersey. I booked a rental car and then searched for hotels near the interview location finally settling on a boutique hotel in Asbury Park, New Jersey named appropriately, *The Asbury*. It looked like a chic hotel with a rooftop bar, and by the lobby, it had a cool lounge that even had pinball machines and board games according to the pictures on their website. This seemed like my kind of place, and most importantly, it was by the ocean and situated only a few minutes from the interview. As promised, Jordie had e-mailed me the details. I was meeting with Jordie first and then the Managing Director, Steve Fletcher. Steve, according to Jordie, was apparently the right hand man to the CEO, but the two of them traveled all the time and Steve was the only one available to meet with me. Jordie had indicated I shouldn't worry, and they have a very streamlined interview process and pride themselves on candidate experience and that they would only bring me in that one day, and then they will make decisions within the week. I was thankful for that because I would hate for them to call me to come back in and be a flight away to have to get back there. I spent some time googling Steve and Jordie and learning as much as I could about the company to prepare before finally falling to sleep.

I didn't even bother to call my father to tell him of my plans. He wouldn't even notice I was missing since he was away on set. I got up at the crack of dawn to pack a suitcase, taking way too long to figure out what clothes to bring. At least it was summer and the weather was warm. I felt mischievous and sneaky as I dragged my suitcase into the elevator and down to our main living area. I had to remind myself that I was a young adult now and I could make decisions for myself. I took a quick look around and avoided any of my father's staff. I was forced to tell the security guard so he could let my Uber in the gate and just told him I had a last minute weekend trip and would be back early next week. Luckily, he didn't inquire further.

I flew out early on Saturday and the Uber successfully got me to LAX, the busiest airport in Los Angeles. I could have easily flew out of Van Nuys' private airport on my father's private jet but then I would have to let him know and I wanted to avoid that. I was on my way, with huge sunglasses to avoid recognition. I could feel the stares from people wondering if I may be important. I drifted off to sleep and had thoughts of a new life for myself. I only awoke when the captain announced we were approaching Newark International Airport in Newark, New Jersey. With the time zone difference, it was already mid-afternoon in New Jersey when I finally landed. I retrieved my luggage, got my rental car and hopped on the Garden State Parkway to find my way to Asbury Park. Asbury Park was about one hour from Newark and I couldn't contain my excitement as I pulled off the highway and onto the side streets that took me into the Jersey Shore towns. I pulled into this eclectic town and immediately noticed how the town was colorful, fun and had a vibe of artistry as I passed surfboard welcome signs and unique businesses. I drove by trendy restaurants and shops and in a small park I could see there was a crowded craft vendor event set up and then finally I drove a little further and hit Ocean Avenue catching a glimpse of the ocean behind their extensive boardwalk. I pulled up to *The Asbury* to the valet parking and got out of my car. The hotel was absolutely stunning and friendly. As I checked in to start my two-night stay, it was already almost dinner time. The front desk told me they have a 4,300 square foot rooftop with magnificent views of the ocean and this evening was movie night. For only $7.00 at sundown, you got free popcorn and a soda and could sit on bean bags or beach chairs and watch a movie under the stars. I couldn't help but think that if I got this job, I would have to have an event at *The Asbury*. I ordered some room service and settled into my room and then went up to the rooftop for movie night. I was always a little weary going to these types of things by myself so I felt nervous as I took the elevator to the rooftop. Their rooftop was transformed into a drive-in movie style outdoor theater complete with a concession stand. I took my free popcorn and drink and sat towards the back in a beach chair. They were playing a John Hughes movie, "*Pretty in Pink*", one of my favorites about two people that fall in love but are from different sides of the track. I could relate with the character "Blane" as he grew up privileged and so did I.

Out of the corner of my eye, I saw a group of guys there for movie night as well. You could tell they were locals and this was probably just the first stop for them before heading out to the nightclub scene or the infamous *Stone Pony* bar to see a concert. They chose some beers and popcorn from the concession stand and took seats on bean bag chairs around the side of the venue to be closer to the bar is my guess. One man, in particular, was tall and lean with blonde hair and blue eyes and was just genuinely handsome, and I couldn't help but notice him immediately. He looked like a Californian surfer and was exactly my type. It felt kind of lonely to be here by myself but it became so crowded that no one could tell who was with each other as the movie began. I was looking forward to the fact that I had the whole day to explore tomorrow before the interview on Monday. I let the ocean air fill my lungs and got lost in the world of John Hughes and his romantic story. As the movie ended, I thought to myself that I could fit in here. No one looked twice at me wondering who I was. For the first time in my life, I blended in.

After a good night's sleep, I was up early on Sunday morning and took a drive along the coast to the beach towns south of Asbury Park. I wanted to explore and also remember a little from the time I spent here growing up with my father when we visited. He still had his house in Spring Lake, but I didn't even tell him I was coming here and didn't want the staff to report to him that I was in New Jersey. He was off on a movie set and wouldn't even know I was gone sadly. I drove through the next town over from Asbury Park called Ocean Grove. This town was also very artsy and the roads were lined with Victorian style homes and a unique little village called "Tent Village" where people literally lived in tents. But, it's not what you would think. The canvas-like structures had the front part of these homes made into an actual tent and then the back was a more solid structure. They had electricity and actually looked comfortable and adorable. I peeked in as much as I could to see bohemian style, full kitchens and bedrooms. It wouldn't be suitable to live all year round but it was summer and the perfect time to feel the ocean breeze in their home in a unique way. I could feel a great sense of community in this little village and I don't think they minded all of the curiosity seekers who drove or walked by their humble but beautiful homes. I was hoping if I got this job and moved here that I would eventually meet someone who lived in Tent Village because I was dying to see what it was like inside these little, unique homes. I grabbed breakfast at an outdoor café in town and sat down to watch the families riding their bicycles, met several friendly dogs on walks, and then headed back to my car to explore the next beach town.

When I arrived in Bradley Beach, I knew I had found my home. This cute little town was located right between Ocean Grove and another sweet town called Avon-by-the-Sea. If I got this job, Bradley Beach was where I wanted to live. It still had an element of art but it was more low-key. It was quiet and family oriented. Main Street in Bradley Beach was lined with restaurants, bakeries and interesting shops. There was a park at the center of town next to a train station that went into New York City. There was a schedule of events hosted in the park displayed including a weekly farmer's market, and last night they had a live band and local vendors set up to shop. The town had every kind of restaurant imaginable too. There was Chinese, Thai, Japanese, Italian, Mexicali, Greek, Jamaican and Mediterranean. There was a beautiful bakery with fresh breads and cannoli's lining the windows. I grinned from ear to ear when I saw the adorable pet grooming place which reminded me how badly I wanted a dog one day. As I took a turn down 4th Avenue, I passed cute homes with wraparound porches and finally hit the ocean. It was much quieter here than Asbury Park. There was a boardwalk for jogging, bike-riding and walking to enjoy the ocean scenery, a children's playground on the beach complete with monkey bars and swings as well as a miniature golf business for families to enjoy. They had Bocce Ball too and I wondered how to play as I saw friends and families out there throwing balls and having a nice time. The beaches were crowded already and there was nowhere to park. I decided to drive back to Main Street and grabbed a brochure from a real estate office to see what was available in town when the realtor, Patrick, came over and introduced himself. I told him I am looking for a two to three bedroom condo or townhouse and he said he happened to be on his way to show one on Ocean Avenue if I wanted to follow and get a quick peek before his guests were to arrive in about 15 minutes. As we walked to our cars, he asked what my budget is and mentioned this one that we are going to see is going for $950,000. He apologized if that was out of my range but I didn't flinch. I told him I was "open", which he probably thought meant I am being nosy and couldn't afford it. Little did he know!

I followed Patrick back over to the crowded Ocean Avenue and pulled into an ocean-front complex of about twenty condominium units. What was nice is if you lived here, you still had a garage to pull your car into and a storage unit as well. The building had an elevator and a swimming pool for its residents. The best thing about it was the fact that it was ocean front, hence the price. Looking at this view though every day, would be worth it. The unit opened into a living area that I would describe as a great room with high ceilings and a fireplace and a deck in the front accessible through sliding doors that was set up with chairs and a table and small grill and I imagined this as a great place where you could have a glass of wine or a cup of coffee and look out at the amazing view. I closed my eyes for a moment and thought of myself sitting here with a coffee in the early morning listening to the seagulls and watching the bicyclists and joggers going by to the sounds of the waves crashing on the shore. I came out of my daydream and entered back inside. Adjacent to the living room was the kitchen. It had bright white cabinets with a few stained glass cabinet doors, granite grey counters and a light grey ceramic tiled floor. It felt open and airy as the sunlight hit the yellow and blues of the stained glass. There was a long kitchen table that sat between the great room and the kitchen that could host a nice dinner party even without the formal dining room. A laundry room and small bathroom were on this level and there was a spiral staircase all the way in the back that led to a private loft in the back that served as an office or guest room. The main set of stairs took you to another landing where you could again have another living room space if you wanted, and the hallway behind had two bedrooms each with their own on-suite bathrooms and walk in closets. The Master Bedroom also had a small deck off of it to sit out and see the ocean. The unit gave exclusive access as well to a rooftop lounge area with assigned section per owner with beach chairs and small enclosed area to hang out in and keep things like a mini-fridge or alcohol. This place was absolute heaven. I felt like everything was aligning for me but didn't want to get too ahead of myself either.

I told Patrick I had a job interview tomorrow and if I got this job, I would pay cash by the end of the week. Patrick's eyes lit up with excitement as I took his business card and gave him my cell phone number before heading out just as the other couple had arrived to look at it. I just hoped they didn't beat me to taking this place. It was almost lunch time but I rode a little further up the busy and bustling Ocean Avenue, watching the surfers, sun bathers and families enjoying the day and I finally arrived at the gates of my father's home in Spring Lake. I could see people tending to the grounds, and the home looked immaculate. My father's home was ocean front. It had a huge outdoor area complete with tennis courts and volleyball nets as well as a swimming pool of course. It was by far one of the prettiest homes in all of Spring Lake and yet no one was there. It was always empty. I think the last time I was there was in high school for three weeks. And, during that time my father stayed maybe four nights total. I don't think he has been back since that time either. I could stay here for free and give the staff someone to worry about. But, you never have alone time when you have a staff and they know everything you do including when you come home at night and who you are with. It's not what I wanted when it was really privacy I desired right now but I did have an urge to want to go inside. I could see the large chandelier glistening in the sun and décor was so different from Los Angeles with a more laid back and relaxing feel. I still remembered my bedroom with the pale yellow walls, king size bed with a white down comforter that I would sleep soundly in after a long day at the beach surfing. I realized how spoiled I had always been and yet I still wasn't happy. Most people would be on top of the world. What was wrong with me?

I headed back to Asbury Park and valet parked my car and headed back to my room. I ordered lunch in and started studying up on the company and their recent events so that I could talk intelligently in my interview tomorrow. I was really nervous. I realized that I REALLY wanted this. I wanted that condo, and I wanted this job. For the first time in my life, I felt like I could obtain my own life on my terms. I had to nail this interview. I texted Claire and filled her in on my adventures and then took a nap before heading to the lounge to grab a light meal and a drink. I walked through the lounge near the lobby and people-watched and then stopped in the gift shop before heading back to my room for the night. I had to get up early, check out and head over for the interview so I wanted to get a good night's sleep, although, I tossed and turned thinking of how invested I felt already in this new life. It felt so freeing to be here with no one bothering me. Deep down I knew this was meant to be for me. I needed to be on my own, standing on my own two feet. I needed to not take for granted the money I had at my fingertips and actually make a difference.

At 5:00 a.m., my alarm clock went off and I had no problem racing out of bed and into the shower. I had to look perfect. I wanted this job more than anything. And, getting this job was not only for myself but to make a difference. I put on a modest but beautiful black dress with a grey jacket and stiletto heels. I wore my long blonde hair clipped back and wore light, simple make-up. I was interview-ready as I packed up my suitcase and grabbed my personal belongings and headed to the lobby to check-out and retrieve my car. I stared out at the ocean and took a deep inhale to feel the Atlantic Ocean air in my lungs one more time before they pulled around with my rental car. I headed over to a Starbucks nearby to grab a coffee and breakfast before heading over to Shore Events. I didn't need to be there till 8:30 a.m. but here I was, forty-five minutes early, sitting in my car. The parking lot was somewhat empty but that was typical in this line of business. It wasn't a 9a-5p type of job. You had to work some nights and weekends and while you were in the office, you were often running around too. It was one of the reasons I loved this field. I liked to move around and be in different places, seeing various people and not handcuffed to my desk.

I decided to go in about ten minutes early so that I could show I was motivated but not overly anxious (although I hoped no one saw me sitting in the car for the last half hour to forty-five minutes waiting with baited breath). I checked in with the receptionist and took a seat in the lobby next to a cute café and began staring at fashion magazines that had been sitting on the table to try and take my mind off the interview and calm my nerves. At about 8:35 a.m., a serious-looking woman comes over to greet me. She introduces herself to me as Jordie and brings me to her office on the 2nd floor and this woman gets right down to business going over my resume and education. There was no small talk about weekends or finding the office easily. I could tell she was going to be hard to win over. She moved on from my resume and started asking me questions about events that I have hosted, and then drills me with scenarios of events gone wrong to see how I would handle. I don't think she even cracked a smile but I tried not to get discouraged. After the wrath of Jordie, I was brought up to the 6th floor to meet with Steve Fletcher, the Managing Director. Jordie excused herself and let his assistant know I was here. About fifteen minutes later, Steve's door opened and two employees walked out and I was finally invited in. Unlike Jordie, Steve was full of energy and very friendly. He talked incessantly about this company and what they stand for. His questions only focused on why I wanted to work here and he asked me how many times I had given back to the community. That was easy for me. Although I am sure that Jordie was wearing her "human resources" hat and asking me the basic 101 questions of being a good employee, showcasing dependability and experience in my craft, Steve was much easier to talk to and so was talking about giving back. I told the countless stories of growing up in Los Angeles and all of the amazing things I did to support the community. I confided in Steve that working in Los Angeles was amazing but that this humanitarian focus is what drew me to Shore Events. I wanted to make a difference and I made it clear that I wanted to work here. I felt like Steve believed me and saw my value. I wasn't so sure about Jordie though and I could only hope I won her over. After I left Steve's office, I stopped back down to thank Jordie but she wasn't there. I left a handwritten note with her assistant asking if I should wait, but she told me Jordie had back to backs and I was welcome to go.

I could finally breathe again as I exited the building and walked to my car. My fate was in their hands now and all I could do is head back home and hope for the best. I had a few hours before I had to fly back out to California so I headed back over to the coast and stopped this time in the same town where Shore Events was located, West Long Branch, to an area called Pier Village. I ate lunch and walked around the shops. This cute beachside town had an arcade, gym, winery, cute trendy clothing stores, and an amazing looking ice cream store. I crossed the street real quick as well to see the ocean one last time before I would head to the airport. I wondered if this view would become one I would soon get used to, or if it was back to California and my father's home for now. If this didn't work, I would have to come up with Plan B but figured I may as well wait and see first before I put my brain into overload. Claire texted me to check in as did the realtor Patrick. I texted back Patrick and asked if the other people liked the home and he said it was a little too pricey for them so it's still available. I told him I would call him by the end of the week once I had heard about the job. I called Claire and filled her in as I headed back out onto the open road towards the airport. I could be a Jersey girl for sure if given a chance I thought and I smiled. For now though, I was headed back to La La Land.

Chapter 2
Goodbye California

It was late on Monday when I arrived back in California. With all the excitement of my interview I had forgotten to call out at work unfortunately. I basically just didn't show up today but funny enough, I didn't even have a missed call from them. Like I said, they really only cared about my last name and this was certainly proof of that. I texted my boss to tell them I was sick and had been asleep all day. I knew I didn't have to but I felt it was the right thing to do and they just responded feel better and see you tomorrow. When I arrived back at my house, there was a text from Bennie wondering where I was and a couple of missed calls from him that finally showed up on my phone from when I had been in flight. While my father wasn't around to notice, Bennie noticed everything. Bennie was practically family and had been with me since birth. I told him I went away for the weekend but I am back and fine and I could tell he was relieved. Bennie was off on the set with my father as well, yet he knew I was gone. He actually took the time to keep tabs on me and make sure I was o.k. I decided to take advantage of the rest of my unofficial day off and worked out in our fitness center and then took a dip in the pool that no one ever seemed to use. I floated on my back, staring up at the sky wondering what lied ahead for me. I enjoyed a moment of peace and quiet but I also felt very alone. I wrapped myself in a towel and headed in to take a shower and go to bed.

When I finally lay in my bed though, I was restless. I pulled out my iPad and began doing some searches on living in New Jersey. This may not even happen, yet I wanted to be prepared and continue on with my dreaming. I thought about movie night at *The Asbury* hotel and that handsome man I had seen. I longed to be in a relationship but I just couldn't find anyone I could trust in this town. I closed my eyes and thought of the attractive man from the movie night and I finally fell asleep until my alarm clock went off and it was back to work. When I arrived at my office in Beverly Hills, the team was mostly there on their phones or computers. My co-workers said hello and I slid into my desk with not even one comment about me not calling out the day prior. We were working on multiple events this week, but I suddenly had no motivation to do them and I just prayed this other job would work out. If not, I wasn't even sure if I could continue here. I was just miserable. I started writing some notes on my "Plan B". First step is to quit this job and leave it all behind. Second step is to look at creating a charity. I could run and manage it. Maybe I could honor my mother in some way. It had been so long that I couldn't even remember what it was like to look into her eyes or hold her hand. I could start a foundation helping others or a scholarship program. There had so be something I could do with all that I had been given. I should be working but I just couldn't focus.

Tuesday afternoon, I was sitting at my desk at work counting the minutes to when I could leave when my cell phone rang with a New Jersey number. I excused myself and walked as fast as I could outside to answer in private as my heart beat a million miles a minute. It was Steve from Shore Events. "*Alexandria, this is Steve. How are you?*" I quickly responded "*Doing better now that I am hearing from you and the team at Shore Events. It was so great meeting you and I am hopeful you have good news for me*." I hoped I didn't sound too confident but my goal was to make it known that I wanted this. I was thankful he couldn't see me and my red cheeks as I grasped the phone for dear life and paced back and forth. "*Well, I do, we would love to have you join the team effective the Tuesday after Labor Day weekend. It's about three weeks from now. Jordie has the salary and details and she is going to e-mail them to you with an offer letter but I wanted to personally call you and offer you the role.*" I tried to sound calm but excited even though inside I felt like screaming hallelujah. I didn't even know the salary but I didn't even care. "*I am so thrilled Steve. I will look over the offer but I am truly excited to accept and join the team. Thank you so much for this opportunity and I promise, I won't let you down*" I answered full of enthusiasm. Steve and I spoke for a few more minutes and then I made my way inside and resigned on the spot and didn't tell them why or where I was going. All they cared about when I told them I was leaving is if I would still come to their events to support them. I thought "*wow*" inside my head as this was confirmation to what I knew deep down that who I am is the <u>only</u> reason they hired me. It had helped their events to have my last name involved. I didn't give a notice, grabbed my stuff, said a few goodbyes, and left forever. I was never going to look back.

I headed back to my car texting Claire that the plans were in motion for me to officially become a Jersey girl. She was happy for me but sad to see that I would be moving so far away. Her comment made me wonder if I was doing the right thing for a moment. I suddenly felt fright mixing in with my excitement. I told Claire that it was probably temporary but in my heart I wasn't so sure it was. I sat in my car for a brief moment wondering what I was doing and if I was indeed making the right decision. I could always back out and say the offer didn't meet my expectations. But then again, I wanted this and I kept on telling myself that this is temporary. I don't have to stay forever if I don't like it. I could run back to Daddy and the comforts of Beverly Hills. I calmed myself down enough to be excited again. I needed to do this…for me. Now, I had to break the news to my father and his staff. But, the first thing I did was text Patrick to draw up papers for a full price offer to my little piece of Jersey Shore heaven in Bradley Beach, NJ and Patrick was thrilled. I would rather pay a million dollars for a condo and delay sharing the news with my father sadly. I worked with Bennie on my father's team to help me break the news to my father and coordinate the move and getting the condo as quickly as possible. While Bennie got our real estate lawyer to chat with Patrick, I called my father to tell him that I was moving across the country. Bennie seemed excited for me but I could see the look of fear in his eyes too. He would finally have to let me go and I too would have to let him go. He knows I am an adult but our bond is so close I could sense the hurt in voice.

It took a while for me to get my father on the phone. He was on set and often busy. I finally got him in between takes and his first words were "this better be good" not "oh my – you never call me on set…is everything o.k." but it didn't surprise me by his initial reaction. I always felt like I was in his way. I was something he was forced to deal with but I never really was sure if he wanted to deal with me or just had to. I took a deep breath and blurted it out. I told my father about my decision to try this job and to get away from Hollywood for a bit where I could grow as my own person. I told him I already accepted it and had found a condo that I wanted to purchase and that I had looped in Bennie on all. My dad seemed to take it well. I assumed Bennie already gave him a heads up too. He said he thought it would be good for me, wished me congratulations, and said that he was proud of me. So, I guess he wasn't going to try and stop me. He really couldn't, since I was an adult but his response sounded cold and almost calculated. I knew he was on set and being pulled in a million directions so maybe it just had to sink in. I wasn't sure but with me moving thousands of miles away, I guess he should realize that it wouldn't make a difference because even living in the same house we never spent time together. He always put work first and the truth is we never saw each other anyway. This conversation was easier that I thought it would be. I loved my father but I just needed so much more from him that he wasn't capable of giving.

Time flew by over the next couple of weeks but my father did come home a few times from the set to see me before my move. I knew it was hard for him to do that so I think deep down he really will miss me after all. He asked me a few times if I was sure I wanted to do this but I confirmed I was. I told him I could always sell the condo and quit if it doesn't work out and he agreed it made since to take the chance. These three weeks that I had were so busy with preparations that I didn't have any time to enjoy the company of the people I cared about. Moving across the country is a huge process and the only thing I didn't have time to do was ship my car out there and decided to just buy one once I got there or even lease it, which is something I have never done before. I had been so focused on picking out furniture for my new place, and packing my clothing and personal items that I had totally forgot about my vehicle. It was kind of an important detail to overlook but I would figure it out and my father told me I could always grab one of the cars from his home in Spring Lake if I needed to.

Before I knew it, my three weeks were up and it was time for me to leave California, at least for a little while, to go on this new adventure. I could be in New Jersey for six months, six years or a lifetime. I wasn't sure what the future held but this was something I had my mind set on. Goodbye California and hello to New Jersey! Although, I still hold California deep in my heart. This was and still is my home and where I grew up. It is and always will be a part of me. I started to have a few doubts but the ball is in motion and I knew deep down this was the path I was meant to be on.

I took one long last look around as I heard the beeping of the car service waiting to take me to the Van Nuys airport to board my father's private jet from California to New Jersey. I stared out at the in-ground pool lining the perfectly manicured grounds and watched the sun reflecting on the water for a few peaceful moments. I gazed out at the tennis courts being cleaned by our groundskeepers and couldn't recall the last time anyone had even used them. I brought my attention inside and looked at our maid vacuuming the white carpeted living room with minimalistic furniture. I knew I would be back for the holidays but going to live across the country was my dream, and a temporary escape from my life as I knew it. It wasn't an escape from the blessings I had been given because of my father's success, but more of a personal escape to find my true purpose in life. I got a little nervous as I took one last look and mentally convinced myself of the reasons why going to New Jersey made sense. I picked somewhere still close to the beach because I grew up at the beach in California, and the salt water is in my blood. I had spent time in New Jersey. My father had many houses including two on the Jersey Shore that I think he has been to all of three times. I am about to venture to something new. It felt like starting over in a lot of ways. I am happy in this moment, and deep down I know I am the lucky one who can always go back to my lavish home and pick up the pieces if I need to.

One of my father's many bodyguards, Bennie, was there to see me off at least because I knew my father wouldn't take the time. He was off on his latest movie set as always. I hugged Bennie and could feel his nervousness in the hug. He held me tightly, and it felt like he was the one letting his little girl go. I hopped in the car service and rolled down the car window as we pulled out of our gated driveway and onto the road. I couldn't help but stare at the road and know that I was on a new journey and I was excited for it. I was anxious to be away from California for a little while, and go somewhere no one knew me. I convinced myself one last time that it was the fresh start I am looking for.

Bennie followed my car service to the airport. He helped me out of the car and with my bags. I said goodbye to Bennie and boarded the plane.

He was like a dad to me. He has been with me since I was born. He is always watching the house, our family but mainly he seems to be assigned to watch me. He was always in my shadow. I think it would be harder on Bennie that I was leaving more so than my own father. It's nice my father feels I need protection I guess since he is so famous, but I would rather my father spend a few minutes talking to me more than twice a year instead of hiring someone to do it for him. I always thought fathers protected their little girls and treated them like princesses. This isn't necessarily the case for me. I grew up in the Hollywood Hills. My birthday parties were featured in People Magazine when I was little. That all changed after my mother overdosed on drugs when I was eight years old. After that, the magazines just questioned what would happen to me. Will Alexandria turn out like her mother? Who is going to raise Alexandria with her father's busy schedule? It was always a strange feeling as a kid to see a magazine with your face on it. Mostly I was shielded from it. It's not like I spent time in grocery stores shopping. We had people to do that.

Growing up in California was amazing for the most part. I went to prestigious private schools and spent a lot of my time at the beach, mainly surfing and hanging out with friends. A lot of celebrity kids can get into a life of privilege and trouble. But after losing my mother, I knew I would never go down that road. I saw the pain it caused. My father was never the same after he lost my mother. He used to be around more. We did things as a family and he would never in a million years have missed a holiday or my first day of school when she was here. After my mom died, my father threw himself into his work. He did one movie after another and his career was on fire. My father was #1 on the Forbes' Wealthiest Actors list and the most in demand actor of the time. I knew he did it to distract from the pain but his thriving career impacted his time with me. He was too busy to be as involved with me and I would only see him in passing for many years. He pretty much missed my teen years and I would be lucky if I saw him more than once or twice per month. He basically knew nothing about me or what I was doing. I overheard him tell Bennie once that looking at me was like looking at my mother. We looked exactly alike except she was a lot taller than me. We had the same big blue eyes, the same long blonde hair, and I think looking at me was almost painful for my dad and he avoided me because of it which broke my heart.

Growing up, I hid my loneliness by throwing myself into school and activities. I was too busy doing gymnastics and cheerleading to focus on trouble or worry about my father and his lack of presence in my life. If my father had paid any attention, I could have possibly done gymnastics professionally. My best skillset was the floor. I could do a double twisting full and a standing full. I went to a gym but mainly just taught myself in the countless hours alone as a kid in a backyard the size of Walt Disney World. I had multiple trampolines and a full gym at my access. Despite my prestigious and private high school, they didn't have a gymnastics team so I did cheerleading there. I fell in love with the sport because I still got to do my tumbling skills, and being a small person, I was the flyer or top girl. I went to college at Pepperdine University and continued cheering there as well. After four years at a school located on the coast in Malibu, California, I was ready to remove the privilege I had become so accustomed to and venture out on my own.

California had been good to me and I grew up wealthy and happy for the most part. Bennie kept me grounded and involved with the community giving back. He taught me the true value of kindness and being a human being. But all in all, I was alone. I never felt a part of the Hollywood scene. I knew I had many doors that could easily open for me. It was all who you know, and I could easily get roles and follow in my father's footsteps. Maybe then we would have something in common. Maybe then, he would finally notice me. But, I didn't think I wanted that lifestyle. The egos and money in this town were ridiculous. It was hard to find people you could really trust that didn't want something from you. All people wanted was to be seen with you for fame and fortune.

My father collected houses like some people collect figurines or baseball cards. There are so many people who could never afford a house or even put food on the table for their families, and here we are with houses all over the world and tennis courts that have never even been used. I knew I could never fully embrace this overindulgent lifestyle. I was grateful for this life but kindness was the only way I could ever really accept all of this. Bennie and I often gave back to the community. He is the one who taught me the art of giving. We fed the homeless and volunteered at soup kitchens growing up. I knew some day when all of this money became mine that I was going to give most of it away. I wanted to set up a scholarship for kids who wouldn't ever have dreamed of being able to afford to go to college or do something to help stop hunger or homelessness. I didn't know what I would do but I knew it wouldn't be selfish. Even if I found my own success someday, kindness was going to be a part of my life in every way. It was through kindness that I had always been my happiest.

My father, on the other hand, focused on possessions. He was known for his focus on wealth, his contract negotiations getting heated and most of all for his on-set behavior. He was a true diva in every sense of the word. He would yell at staff if things weren't perfect. And, when on a movie set, his list of needs was over ten pages long, even if he would only be there for one day. The media was all over him for this, but he felt he was above everyone and it did little to deter him. He had lost the meaning of being a human being. He looked at himself as a superior to everyone and everything. Even for myself, his own daughter, I felt like I was a possession to him. He has assigned someone to look over me. He was never around but in interviews acted like we were thick as thieves. He would talk about my education and my focus on charitable causes as if he were involved. It made him look good and at the end of the day, that is all he cared about.

I looked into the compact mirror that I pulled from my purse to check my mascara hadn't run down my cheeks from my goodbye with Bennie as the plane took off. My reflection back was the spitting image of my mother. I had the same long, wavy blonde hair and bright blue eyes. I was only 5 feet 2 inches and about 100 pounds though so despite some good genetics, I didn't think modeling would be in my future as it had been for my mother back in the day. Still, I was blessed with what Hollywood would want and I had all the connections. But, I just wanted a normal life right now. I didn't ever need money. My father had enough money and I had enough trust funds to last a lifetime. How many people my age could pay cash for a million dollar condo?

I closed my eyes on the plane and drift off into a world of dreams. My mother's genes had all been passed on to me, and my startling transformation into her twin had been too much for my father to bare. Not many people remembered my mother as her career was cut short with her untimely death and it was probably a good thing I looked nothing like my father, who everyone knew. He was the most famous man in the world. He was People Magazine's "Sexiest Man Alive" twice! He dated other A-Listers and all of his movies were blockbusters. I was proud of him but all I really wanted was for him to notice me. All of these accolades in his life were never going to be as important as being my father, and I just wished he would remember that. His Oscars and Golden Globes lined the mantle of his office but he needed to look no further than in my direction to find his #1 fan. I loved my father but only he could figure out what was more important to him – his career or his family. He was all I had besides Bennie. And I couldn't help but wonder when his career dies down, where will he turn his direction? Would it ever be directed towards me? I was tired of waiting and just needed to start my own life and hope that someday he would love me the way I needed him to. And, I hoped he would remember how good it would feel to give back and make a difference.

I stare out the plane window and am anxious for what lies ahead at Shore Events now that college is over, and I am out of the meaningless event company that I worked for in Los Angeles. Shore Events was a marketing agency that had an arm focused on non-profit event support. They had offered me a Marketing Manager role where I would work with the local Jersey Shore towns on managing events that offered a way to give back to the community or organizations locally. It was the perfect scenario for me. I was working managing events but was able to focus on giving back. There was a team of us that worked together and I prayed that we would all get along. I had nothing tying me back to California anymore except for some friends, Bennie, and of course my father. I didn't have a boyfriend or anything like that to worry about. It was a complete fresh start into the unknown and I just hoped I would fit in and that no one would know who I was.

I was so excited that I had purchased the condo of my dreams in Bradley Beach, New Jersey overlooking the ocean. I kept looking at pictures of the condo as we flew to New Jersey. It was a two/three bedroom, three bathroom condo with ocean views for miles. It was probably considered a lot in terms of price for someone who just graduated college not that long ago, but I was just going to tell people I was renting if they asked. Aside from a college dorm, this would be my first time really being on my own and owning a piece of real estate as well. I couldn't wait! Looking out at the ocean each morning was a view I knew I would never get tired of. It would also remind me of California and make me feel at home.

When I landed in Newark, New Jersey, I had arranged for a car service to be there to pick me up since my car hadn't made it over to California. I made sure it wasn't a limo so that it looked at least somewhat normal. I was starting to have anxiety about not having a car and work being only a day or two away. I guess worst case scenario, I could rent a car for a week or two, grab a car from Spring Lake belonging to my father, or take an Uber. My father had arranged a moving service and assistant to go into my condo and bring all my belongings – or should I say his team had arranged this for me. I was upset because if I was going to do this on my own, then I really was going to do this on my own and didn't need them here. When I got to my condo, I asked them to leave. They had done the hard work by the time I got there anyway, carrying everything up to my place and putting together some furniture I had ordered but I was fully capable of putting away my own personal stuff. I couldn't help but notice the team had left a set of keys with a small bow on it on the kitchen counter. I knew immediately they were car keys. I walked down to the garage to see a new BMW sitting there. I knew it was from my father. You would think I should be thrilled but this car just made me look like a rich kid, and wasn't going to help me appear normal in any way whatsoever. I didn't want to seem ungrateful so I texted my father and thanked him. This was nice but such a typical move for Alexander Thompson. He was in more movies than Tom Cruise but my last name was generic enough that people wouldn't put two and two together, and I hoped that no one knew who I really was. I secretly wished he would've used a different name for his acting career so that I could be more incognito.

I was never in the spotlight really so why were people so interested in my life? I did have a page on TMZ dedicated to me but it was mostly inactive because I mainly fly under the radar. I stayed away from movie premieres and celebrity friends so I could only hope my identity would remain a secret. My parents named me Alexandria after my father since they probably wanted a son but that didn't happen, so it was the closest they could get to Alexander. At Shore Events, I would go by Ria. No one in my life had ever called me that. Lexi, Alexandria or Lex were the only names anyone had ever called me. Going by Ria was the only way I could at least hide a little bit from my full first name and help eliminate anyone finding out my true identity. It would be an adjustment to be called Ria though. I hope when someone calls my name that I remember to respond.

I only had the weekend to put my condo together but I took great pride in emptying every box myself that hadn't been managed by the moving team my father had sent. Everything I had purchased for this condo, I had bought it on my own with no help from my father although I guess a lot of that money ultimately came from him through my trust. As I opened another box, I was elated and nostalgic as I pulled out my most prized possession. It was a framed photo of my mother from her modeling days. It was a famous shot of her called "Sunsets and Margaritas" because she was on a beach as the sun was setting while modeling for Sports Illustrated and held a margarita in her hand. It was her most famous photo from back in the day many years ago. I missed her terribly but at least this photo was when she was healthy and happy. I was a small child at the time but don't even remember being at the photo-shoot with her. I had the photo blown up and framed it and hung it proudly in my living room above the fireplace. I smiled as I poured myself a glass of white wine and sunk into my new living room couch admiring my mother's beauty. This was really happening! I was on my own and it felt good. I was done unpacking by Sunday afternoon. I had planned on buying a car but could scratch that off my list thanks to my father. I knew he meant well but again, his way of showing me attention was through the power of money.

In my bedroom that evening, I fell into bed from exhaustion and my body ached. I still managed a smile as I realized that this was one of the first of many nights in my new place. It felt strangely more comfortable than I thought it would. I thought I would feel like I was in a hotel, or staying with a friend. But, it felt like I was home…in my home. And, I was used to being alone. I was nervous but excited for the start of my new job tomorrow but luckily too exhausted from the move this weekend and fell fast asleep. Tomorrow was a new day and I felt like a new person. I had my clothes laid out and ready like a school girl. I slept peacefully and dreamt of my new life in New Jersey. The next morning, I awoke with a smile to my alarm to start my new life. I hopped out of bed and walked out to the balcony and stared out at the Atlantic Ocean. Even at the crack of dawn, people are jogging or walking on the boardwalk, and the sun rising is spectacular. I could get used to this.

Early Monday morning, I pulled into the parking lot of Shore Events. The company was located about twenty minutes from my condo in a town called West Long Branch, New Jersey. The building was brick with a huge sign "SHORE EVENTS" on the lawn. I was way too early but I just sat in my car with a nervous stomach just as I did the last time I was here for the interview. I finally emerged from my car and entered into the lobby and was greeted by the same receptionist from when I interviewed, and she brought me to a conference room to do my new hire paperwork and onboarding. A woman named Jordan Rogers who went by Jordie from Human Resources came in and reintroduced herself to me as if I didn't recall who she was from just a few short weeks ago. She took me on a tour of the building and walked me around to introduce me to the team. Jordie was a thin, brunette woman in her upper twenties. I couldn't help but notice she seemed to look at me from head to toe as if she was judging me or saw me as competition. I tried to brush that off and give her a chance. The Hollywood in me couldn't help but think everyone was out for something. After walking past rows of cubicles and offices, she brought me to a small office where I would sit. She gave me the information to get into my computer and showed me how to use my phone while handing me a printout of the rest of the day's schedule in case I had a hard time getting into my calendar before she disappeared. It was about 10:30 a.m. now and I didn't have anything until 1:00 p.m. so I settled into my office and started going through my e-mails and calendar invites.

A man named Matt poked his head into my office and he looked very familiar to me as he said "*hey new girl*". "*That's me. I am Ria*" I replied and I got up to shake his hand. "*I'm Matt McKinney. I am also a Marketing Manager here and have been here about two years. Let me know if you need anything. I know this place like the back of my hand and we will be working closely together*" he shared as Jordie returned to check on me. "*I see you've met Matt*" said Jordie and Matt quickly left as soon as she arrived, and he almost seemed to run away from her. Maybe he felt the same way about Jordie as I did too I thought and I laughed inside. Matt seemed eerily familiar. I felt like I had met him before. I told Jordie that I was able to get into my computer and that I saw my next appointment was early afternoon so I was going to finish going through my e-mails and grab lunch to be back by the meeting. Jordie left and I sat in my chair and snuck a quick text to Bennie to let him know I was at work and excited. Bennie replied with a heart emoji and "I'm proud of you" and it made my day. I ran back over to the Pier Village area and had lunch at Playa Bowls there. The line was so long I wasn't sure I would make it back in time but I was able to get my bowl and I ate in my car back in the parking lot at work before reemerging.

After lunch, I entered the conference room on my floor, Matt was already there and he smiled at me when I walked in. I sat next to Matt and another girl walked in and sat next to me and introduced herself as Monica Rachels. Monica was a tall, lean girl with brown hair and brown eyes. I noticed Monica had a ring on her finger so she was married. Monica told me that she had been working there for a little over a year and is a Special

Events Manager. I couldn't help but think of the show *Friends* when I heard Monica's name so I told her and she giggled at my comment. Monica and I made small talk with Matt listening to every word. I could tell immediately that Monica and I were going to be friends. She was genuine and had a calm nature about her.

"*So, you moved here from California?*" asked Monica. "*Yes, I went to Pepperdine University there and I am renting over in Bradley Beach, New Jersey*" I responded. "*That's a big move*" replied Monica "*you going to miss the weather for sure but being at the beach will make it feel like home. Do you have family here?*" I swallowed and tried to be casual in my response "*I do not but my dad is out in California and travels a lot to the East Coast for business so I will see him often, but I am pretty much on my own just starting a new chapter I guess.*" I tried to change the subject "*do you live near the office?*" "*I live not too far from you in Avon-by-the-Sea with my husband and a two-year old*" Monica answered showing me a picture of her adorable daughter. "*Let me know if you need anything. Pretty amazing to move across the country.*" She couldn't believe my courage to move across the country by myself. I can see why she would think that. She didn't know that I have basically been by myself my whole life anyway. I was good at hiding that. Other than her looks, the one thing I got from my mother was her optimism. I was a generally happy person despite things happening around me. My mom was the same way when I was little. She was always joyful and easy to be around until drugs took her spirit and eventually her life. People always told me that they liked being around me because I was always a very happy person and full of positivity. That's why I had been a great cheerleader back in the day too. Inside, I had a lot of sadness but I always chose to be positive because I think you can be in control of your own destiny, and I truly believe that. I had always been drawn to things that made me feel content and almost earthy. It's why I loved the peace of the ocean. Being near the ocean brought out the best in everyone. I knew it was in us all to be kind and good people, if we dug deep enough.

The meeting started and we had an ice breaker session as a way to introduce me to the team. Everyone had to go around and name a fun or interesting fact about ourselves. What the heck was I going to say? I am the daughter of Alexander Thompson? Matt went first and shared that he had once been homeless and that he joined the company as a way to give back as he knew what it felt like to have so little. I had a new appreciation for Matt and all he had been through and I stared at him while he told his story in awe. I just couldn't even imagine it. Looks can be deceiving because Matt's blonde hair, blue eyes and surfer look would never give away the upbringing he struggled through. Monica went next and shared that she is obsessed with baking and once considered going to culinary school. Monica mentioned she loves to bake with her daughter just as she did with her own mom growing up. Another co-worker named Jake mentioned he was a star football player in high school and college and almost played professionally, to which Monica rolled her eyes. I cracked a smile at Monica and had to think of something quick to share. I decided to go with something that anyone growing up near the Jersey Shore with so many arcades and boardwalks would love and shared my obsession with Skee-Ball, and that I have never met anyone that could beat me. Matt nudged me and said "*we are definitely going to play Skee-Ball and I am definitely going to be the first person to beat you*" and I laughed and just said "*game on*" and we shook on it.

We then dove into business and one of our first events that we would plan for was an autograph breakfast with the New York Giants with proceeds going to the local children's hospital. I could feel my foot tapping and moving recklessly under the table to contain my excitement. This was a fact I could've easily shared during the ice breaker had I thought of it and that is that I am **obsessed** with football. I was probably the only girl all through high school that didn't answer my phone on Monday nights during Monday Night Football. I loved all sports but I was obsessed with football in particular. My favorite team had always been the New York Giants so being in New Jersey where they play was particularly exciting for me. I had dated a football player in college named Tony. He was the son of a Hollywood producer. We only dated on and off, and he was kind of a jerk now that I think about it. His ego was pretty big and he kind of represented the typical Hollywood brat but at the time, I didn't realize it and he was someone fun to hang out with. We remained friends at least and ultimately, we just had different interests in the end. He was going to take the Hollywood track and despite going to college, was off to auditions that his parents would help set him up with. It's all who you know and it would be pretty easy for him to get some roles and I was sure I would see him on the big screen soon.

Tony was the only real boyfriend I have ever really had. But, in the end, we were just meant to be friends. I had also dated a boy during the summer of my high school years a few times when I stayed at my father's house on the Jersey Shore in a small, upscale town named Spring Lake. I had met Mercer surfing a few times through the years, and we used to hang out a lot on the beach and then used fake driver's licenses to get into Bar Anticipation in Belmar, New Jersey on the weekends. It was more of a summer fling on and off through the years but at a young age a few weeks felt so serious. My father would often have me stay in New Jersey in the summers when he filmed movies in New York City. He basically stayed in the City and on the set and Bennie was with me mainly. Hanging out on the beach, I made lots of local friends, including Mercer. Mercer moved from Spring Lake, New Jersey just a few towns over to another upscale town called Avon-by-the-Sea, New Jersey which is where Monica mentioned she lived. I hadn't thought about Mercer in a long time and I wondered if I would bump into him. I didn't want him to spill the beans on who my father is to any of my co-workers though. I should reach out to him and let him know I am here but our love story ended a long time ago and we were just meant to be friends. And, the distance didn't help maintain it when you live across the country. Still, I owed him a call and it would be nice to know at least someone in the area.

We wrapped up our meeting with getting our assignments and I dove right into work head-first. I couldn't wait to work with the New York Giants. I felt just like the fans I had grown to get annoyed by in California, and remembered it could be fun to look up to the famous. I was excited to get to know Monica, Matt and Jake and already felt comfortable at Shore Events. Each day at work I couldn't wait to get there. This assignment was actually fun and I enjoyed it. And, before I knew it, days had passed at work. And, after working with the team these past few days, I realized that although we were all very different, I could tell we would get along. Monica was a sweetheart and very positive like myself. She had to balance work and family though so she didn't do any late nights so I spent most of my time with Matt. We were both single, and he was so easy to be around. Jake was with us often too but despite being single, he seemed to have a busier social life than Matt and was always going on countless dates and told us of some funny stories of dating disasters too. Jake had a bit of an ego, but deep down I could tell he was a good guy.

After days turned into a few weeks, I couldn't believe I hadn't even missed California or my old life there. I was too busy decorating my condo, learning the area, getting settled at work and working closely with Jake, Monica and Matt on the New York Giants Charity Breakfast and Autograph Signing. Jake had been considered for pro-football and was auditioned to play professionally in the NFL but during his rookie training camp, he was ultimately cut by the New York Giants of all teams. I wasn't sure if he was upset by his career change or if he was happy to just use his past football skills as a way to impress women. But I kind of felt bad he had to do this event knowing he almost had a shot at being a player for them. Jake though seemed more interested in women than anything else. Jake had asked me out a few times already, and I told him to give me a little time to adjust before I run and date a co-worker but he was always relentless. He was always dropping by my office with coffee or joining me (or should I say inviting himself) for lunch. Jake just wasn't my type. His personality was too much for me and he seemed kind of self-centered. It was nice that he liked me but I had zero interest. Luckily, Matt was there too and he always told Jake to back off and leave me alone.

One day, Matt and I were grabbing coffee and talking about the social scene in this area of the Jersey Shore. We were talking about things to do locally for fun and Matt brought up the hotel I had stayed at this summer, *The Asbury*, and their rooftop lounge's movie night in the summers being his favorite thing to do. That was it! I knew he looked familiar. He was the tall, blond haired, blue-eyed man I had seen hanging with friends watching "Pretty in Pink" when I stayed there for the interviews. I knew he looked familiar and he really was as handsome as ever. Our paths had crossed and we didn't even realize it. Part of me hoped deep inside this was fate but I remembered that fate may just be something we see in the movie business. Was it a part of the make believe we see on the screen? I convinced myself to push that thought aside. I couldn't help but have a spark of interest for Matt though. He was the total package. He had faced adversity and won. He liked giving back. And, he was the most handsome man I had ever seen. I tried to just focus on my condo. I had found so many cool and unique shops in all of the little towns around me and purchased things to decorate my condo. I even bought a vintage surfboard and hung it on one of my walls like art.

I just loved anything to do with the beach and wanted to surround myself with it even in my own home.

Late one night, Monica and I had worked late into the evening organizing details for the event. I knew Monica hated working late and being away from her daughter and when we left for the night and arrived at our cars in the parking lot, we quickly noticed she had a flat tire. I offered to drive her home since she lived super close to me and both of us have no clue how to change a tire. When we arrived at Monica's house, I got to meet her husband, Robbie, who owns a landscaping business, and their young daughter, McKenna. They had a cute ranch style home a few blocks from the ocean. McKenna instantly liked me and brought me into the kitchen where she had been happily making chocolate chip cookies with her dad and her grandmother, Colleen. Colleen was Monica's mother and she watched McKenna while her parents worked and Monica had told me how lucky she was to have her mom live locally to help her out. I joined in on the cookie making telling McKenna that I had a special recipe that was my mother's family recipe for butter cookies. I promised her I would come back closer to the holidays, and we could make them together and decorate them. McKenna was thrilled and she hugged me getting flour all over my dress and we laughed. After apologizing profusely for McKenna's handprints all over my dress, Monica asked me how I was liking working at Shore Events as we continued our cookie making. I told her that while it was what I expected in terms of the role, it was much more exciting and rewarding than my prior job. I really enjoyed working on events that had a benefit to helping others and explained that this is why I had taken the job. She quickly agreed and said it's hard to find such a unique combination in a company. She told me I fit in so well with the team and she was happy also to have another female on the team after being surrounded by men on the team for so long, especially a character like Jake. We laughed hard at that and after a lot of cookies were baking in the oven, Monica left with her husband to head back to the office to deal with her tire so I said my goodbyes as well and drove home, noticing flour all over my dress still. I wondered if someday I would have a husband and a child to bake cookies with and I hoped I would. I envied what Monica had. They were a really cute family.

I went into my condo and made myself a small dinner of a simple salad and a small filet of fish that I had marinating in my refrigerator and called Bennie to give him an update. I had been here for a few weeks now and hadn't even heard from my father but I guess I hadn't called him either. But, I was happy and doing o.k. for myself which made me pretty content. I really liked Matt and Monica a lot so far and was excited about work. I guess I like Jake too, although he does drive me a little nuts. Bennie told me he was going to send me a gift soon and I was excited. His gifts weren't typically extravagant and more thoughtful so I was anxious to see what he would send me. He was like a father to me and I smiled as I hung up the phone. I only wished my dad would check in as well but Bennie told me he has a lot going on and that he told him to tell me he is thinking of me. I looked through my recipes in my kitchen before bed and pulled out my butter cookie recipe so that I could have it ready for my future baking date with McKenna. Luckily, I had packed all of my cookie cutters in holiday shapes and I even had this cookie cutter kit from Williams Sonoma that had letters you could slide into the cookie cutter and spell out messages or your name. I knew McKenna would get a kick out of it so I put that in a bag with the recipe and cookie cutters and set it aside. I was looking forward to spending more time with Monica and her family. These were the things I never got to do with a mother growing up, and I couldn't wait to be able to do with my own family someday. The recipe I had was on an old index card in my mother's handwriting. It was discolored and part of the ink smeared probably from messy fingers while baking. I didn't care. It made me think of her when I touched it. I miss her so much.

Chapter 3
MOVIE MELTDOWN

Back in California, I, Alexander Thompson, was doing what I did best by spending my time reading scripts and negotiating movie contracts while sitting in my home office enjoying a brief moment of solitude. The house felt quieter than ever though with Alexandria's move to New Jersey. I wanted to tell her not to go but I knew how terrible a father I had been to her through the years, and I don't think it would've gone well. Granted I wasn't abusive in any way whatsoever but I was just simply never there. When I was married, I was happy. Despite all of the divorces in Hollywood, I knew I had met my life partner in Alexandria's mother, Carissa. We had a whirlwind romance and we both fell hard for each other. We were both young in our careers and when Alexandria was born, my life felt complete. She was the spitting image of my wife and didn't even have an ounce of my looks to her but I could care less. I wouldn't have wanted it any other way. Alexandria carries on the beauty of her mother to this day.

We were like the three musketeers and despite demanding schedules, we always put our little family first. Things changed when Carissa was doing a modeling assignment and had a fall where she had been posing on a ledge. She lost her footing and fell about three feet but landed awkward on her back and side. The pain was tremendous for her. Like Alexandria but a lot taller, Carissa was actually a tiny person. This fall really caused her horrible back pain. Carissa was prescribed OxyContin for the pain. It was only supposed to be for a few weeks to help her heal but after the OxyContin, she was able to get her hands on Percocet and even Vicodin. I was filming a movie in Europe and when I came home to visit, I noticed Carissa's weight loss immediately. She told me she had no appetite and she appeared anxious all the time. I didn't even realize it was related to her back pain and the medication and just thought maybe she was going through a phase. But, when I returned again two weeks later, things seemed worse. She would talk about her pain medication all of the time, and weird packages had come in the mail as if she was ordering medicine through someone. She wasn't following the proper dosages recommended by her doctor either. I had never experienced this before and didn't realize all the glaring signs of addiction being thrown at me. It's something I will always regret.

I had to go back one more time to film and when I came back, I told her we needed to get her some help if this behavior continued. I hired Bennie around the time Alexandria was born but when the drugs started with my wife, I changed his job description to keep an eye on Alexandria. I didn't feel that Carissa was trustworthy and was obviously becoming an addict, but I never in a million years thought that would be the last time I would see her. I think I was in denial and it had been such a short time so I figured it was just a phase and she was dealing with so much pain. About a week later, Carissa was found dead on the bathroom floor from an overdose after taking medicines she had bought off of someone. They hadn't even come from her doctor. I always regretted that I hadn't acted sooner. My life was over now without Carissa in it. Alexandria was so little and I didn't know how to deal with it. Bennie stepped in and took Alexandria under his wing. A part of me died the day I lost Carissa and I always blamed myself for not leaving the movie set and putting her in rehab immediately. I really didn't know the breadth of how bad things were with her but I should have.

My career on the other hand had been on an upward climb, and my personal loss only made people want to help me more. Hollywood is funny that way. When you are down and you come back, people love it. But, I wasn't coming back necessarily, I had already been climbing this mountain with or without the loss of my wife. Her loss only made me devote my time to my work even more. Acting gave me the chance to pretend I was someone else and at this time in my life, I wanted to be someone else more than anything. It was the perfect way for me to sidestep my problems and what had happened to Carissa. I avoided the pain I felt by throwing myself into my career and Hollywood loved seeing my success. It probably wasn't the smartest move but I didn't know how else to deal with it. I was signed to play Superman, an FBI agent, an alien and romantic leads. But these weren't just roles, these were the blockbuster roles that were coveted and all the top actors fought for. I was only doing major releases so that meant about two movies each year. Most movies took about four or five months to shoot and sometimes the elaborate ones took up to eight months. I would be up at 4:30 a.m. every day, in hair and make-up by 5:00 a.m. and worked twelve to fourteen hour days. I filmed anywhere from four to seven days per week depending on what was happening. And, most of my films weren't even shot in Los Angeles bringing me all over the country and the world. I made myself so busy that I didn't have time to think about anything else but work.

Having this career meant so many good things like wealth and fame but it also meant I was never home. I tried to compensate my lack of time with Alexandria by buying homes all over the place. Through the years, Alexandria made comments of how I collected homes like people collect baseball cards but I was buying homes near major cities where I often filmed movies so that she could be near me and I could see her as much as possible. Everything I did was for her but I don't think she saw it that way. Part of my problem is that I never told her. I avoided conflict when

I should have just told her the truth. It would have made her at least feel appreciated and important to me. Then, as time passed as well, I will admit I found myself going deeper and deeper into the self-indulgent lifestyle that this career has afforded me. I looked around my office and at all of the accolades that I have won. While I knew it meant I did my job well and convincingly, it never filled the hole in my heart from losing my wife, and in a way my daughter too. And both of these failed relationships felt like my fault. I just started to block out my feelings and focus on myself. My ego was growing and so was my attitude. I had always felt I could do no wrong and I had gotten such elite status that I felt I deserved to be treated differently and better than everyone else. I was walking closer and closer to the edge of a cliff and if I kept going, I was going to fall off with no one there to catch me.

Alexandria really is my proudest accomplishment. I talk about her wherever I go because I want her to know she is always on my mind. This job keeps me so busy that I don't even have much time to think of anything or anyone but myself. It's true I have my list of demands wherever I go because I have such little time that I just need things to go perfect because I don't have time for any detours. I was auditioning now and reviewing contracts with movies set in the New York area. I wasn't going to tell Alexandria just yet but her old man was finally waking up. My little girl was a grown woman, and I wasn't getting any younger. I wanted to be situated by her as much as I could and be more involved with her life. I was going to do it a little bit at a time so that I didn't overwhelm her. I wasn't sure how she would react if I just suddenly was there every single day of her life. I was nervous though that her stint in New Jersey would be temporary and then I will commit myself to New York and she won't even be there. But, based on what Bennie was telling me, she sounded happy there.

I knew Alexandria was at an age that she could meet someone and get married and push her life in a new direction. I wanted to make sure I was there for it more than I had ever been in the past. Unlike me, Alexandria doesn't have a selfish bone in her body. She has really been influenced by her time with Bennie, who is the same way. Benjamin, who we affectionately call Bennie, has been giving back his whole life. Bennie didn't have family and we had become his life. He is the one who taught Alexandria the meaning of kindness and that even though she had so much, it only meant she could do so much more for others. What Bennie had taught Alexandria and how it impacted who she had become was something I could never repay Bennie for. I would be devastated if Alexandria ever took a path like her mother chose in the end. But, I knew I would never have to worry about that. Despite my lack of presence, Alexandria had grown into a compassionate and kind woman, and I would never be half the person she had become.

I was super interested in this five part movie deal filmed completely in New York. It would put me in the New York City area for a period of about 3 years if I got it. The film was about a man who could time travel. He was an agent who was sent in the past and to the future to help prevent major disasters. Each movie focused on a secret society that he was trying to get involved with to stop the devastating future they would create. The first movie started with this future reality where people had no freedoms and lived in constant fear. It was up to this main character to go back to where it all began in time and spend significant amounts of time in this past world to try to change the future world but by doing so, he risked changing his own life that he had built for himself, including the family that he had created. It was kind of like a *Back to the Future* meets *Hunger Games* but more than anything it had box office appeal that was going to rival the likes of those movies and even *Star Wars*. This was not only good for my career but it would keep me near my daughter for several years. I would still have the long days and hours but when I did have time off, I wouldn't be in another part of the world and for the first time, I could put her first. This was something I should've done a long time ago. Unlike my character who could change the past, I couldn't do that so all I have in my power is to change the present and the future and rebuild my relationship with Alexandria.

The part would've been a shoe-in for me however, I did have an on-set meltdown recently on my astronaut movie causing us to have to do re-shoots in the near future. I was having a hard time dealing with Alexandria leaving and we had this young actor in the film who gave nothing but attitude. He was leaking photos of me to the media where I didn't look my best and I had reached my boiling point and refused to come out of my trailer unless they fired him. The movie was about three quarters of the way done so I cost the film crew money and time by refusing to work. It was unprofessional and unfair what I did to all involved. I let one person's actions dictate the entire film putting it in jeopardy. I now had to do re-shoots over Thanksgiving to make up for the time I had cost them. This on-set antic wasn't going to help me get this other part that I wanted so badly. I had to turn it around and do a lot of schmoozing now where normally I probably wouldn't have had to worry about it if I would've just been a professional and dealt with this actor knowing it was almost over anyway.

My meltdown was a wake-up call for me though. I couldn't go on working all these hours, exhausted all the time and I needed to only pick projects that made that time commitment worth it. I couldn't hold down a relationship because I was never there to even have one. I would just pick up women in general to satisfy me physically, but never took the time to really get to know any of them. From now on, I was going to pick projects I really wanted to do and spend time with people that really meant something to me. I was going to take the time to enjoy the downtime of life more, and hopefully fall in love again one day. What was the point of having all that I do if I never enjoyed any of it? I have tennis courts I never even played tennis on. I have swimming pools that sit there empty and cars that are never driven. I have all of these homes, but I am never at them, and some I haven't been to in more than five years. All I do is work. It's all I have and all that defines me. But, I was ready, just as Alexandria was, to get my life in order. She was out finding herself but I was finally finding myself too.

I was going to do whatever it took to land this time traveler movie role of a lifetime. I was up against some big names in Hollywood though but I knew I would have had this if I didn't have my on-set bad behavior, so I had to put in the extra effort here to get the role. But, I would get it. I would stop at nothing until I did. If my daughter had the courage to find a company that stood for something important, a job that made her happy and focusing on things important to her, and moved by herself across the country to do it, I think I could muster up the courage to talk to this director and lawyer to tell them the reasons for my on-set antics and what I learned from it. It was time for me to communicate more with my business partners, with my daughter but mostly with myself. I may be Alexander Thompson but I need to realize I am just a person too. A person with flaws just like anyone else. It's time to wake up and be a better man.

Chapter 4
FOOTBALL AND FRIENDS

My next door neighbor at my condo complex was an overweight man named Roger. He was a loner and never really spoke to anyone. I noticed he ordered a lot of take out when the pizza or Chinese delivery men passed my doorway to knock on his door. But, mainly I noticed he was often alone. This always bothered me and me wonder about him. I had observed he was always sketching in a pad sitting on his balcony, and could tell he was into art. I knew what it felt like to be alone and found myself drawn to him. I knew he must do well for himself to be living here and maybe he just liked solitude to be able to draw or paint. I mean just looking at this ocean view is enough inspiration for an average person but could only imagine what it could do for an artist's creative juices. I couldn't just stand by and see Roger go through life with no friends though, although he could have a ton of them for all I knew. I was going by my gut feeling and figured I'd find out. I could tell he was a gentle person. The day I had moved into my place, he was kind enough to hold open the elevator for me when I was carrying boxes and even helped me carry one of my boxes to my condo. Other people in my complex were friendly but never offered a helping hand, and I also noticed they just seemed to ignore Roger.

One night after work, I got on the elevator with Roger just as my father had finally called me to see how I was doing. He was only on the phone with me for thirty seconds and then had to run which made a tear stream down my face as I hung up my phone. Roger and I got off the same floor since he lived down the hall from me and he just said "*People suck Ria. Don't let it bother you*" and he turned down towards his place. I yelled "*Thanks Roger*" as I walked down towards my room appreciating his compassionate gesture. I knew Roger was a special person and this moment just reemphasized it.

A few days later, I saw Roger carrying a large drawing from his car and I asked if I could see it and he showed it to me. It was a painting he had done of a building and it was beautifully done. I asked Roger more about his background and he told me that he was an art freak who just loved to draw since a little boy. He told me had majored in Fine Arts at Monmouth University and now paints and sells his paintings through an art dealer, as well doing other art-related jobs for businesses and individuals. He said he mainly worked from home given his line of work. He had the same set up in his place as mine and had used that loft space up the spiral staircase as an art studio. As we walked inside the building, I started smiling so Roger asked me why I was so happy and I told him "*it's Monday.*" He gave a confused look until I explained. It was my favorite night of the week – a Monday which meant Monday Night Football and Monica had invited me to meet up with her to watch the football game at a local bar. I looked at Roger and asked him if he wanted to come hang out with us. Roger said "*I don't know Ria. Would your friends take to me*?" I told him "*It doesn't matter because I've taken to you and I want you to come so come by my condo at 7:00 p.m. and then we can head over together.*" The look on his face made it seem like he would no show but at 7:00 p.m., Roger showed up at my door with perfect punctuality. We decided to Uber so that we wouldn't have to drink and drive. Monica and Robbie were already at the bar when Roger and I walked in. Jake and Matt were there too with a bunch of friends and we all sat together. Jake texted me and asked what was up with my charity case. That really bothered me. I knew Jake had an ego the size of my father's but I had hoped he would be a little more compassionate and non-judgmental about making friends. I just texted him back to shut up and that Roger is a really great guy. Jake responded if he should be jealous and I just texted back "*maybe*."

Matt on the other hand talked to Roger all night. He asked him questions, got to know him and treated him like he would any other human being. Matt, Roger and I did shots and played darts during commercial breaks. At half time, there was a small dance floor and Matt was surprisingly a little daring when he had alcohol in him and his dance stylings consisted of the worm and his own variation of the YMCA to all of our amusement. Matt was touchy, feely with me on the dance floor too. He would put his arms around me and dance closely with me, and this wasn't slow music at this point in the evening. I have never wanted someone to kiss me more in my entire life and I wished I had psychic abilities and could read his mind to see what he thinks of me. Roger took me aside and told me he thinks Matt has a thing for me to which I drilled him like an army sergeant to find out if Matt had confided in him, but unfortunately it was just a vibe that Roger had. But that gave me hope!

We didn't really care about any of the teams playing the game tonight so we spent time just simply having fun. Jake was trying to hook up with every girl at the bar having gave up I guess on me, and also kept trying to drag Matt over there with him. I told Matt he could go but inside I would've died if he did especially if he ended up hooking up with someone in front of me. Matt said he would be back in a minute and was going to just go for a few minutes so that Jake didn't kill him, and I immediately got upset inside as I watched him walk over to the bar with Jake to try and pick up girls. I really had a thing for Matt. I was literally head over heels, butterflies in the stomach for him and one thing was for sure – I had never felt this way in my life. We weren't even together and

I couldn't stand him talking to any other girl but myself. I felt like a crazy person.

As soon as Matt left me, Roger went to the bathroom and I went up to the other bar to order a drink when a man came up right next to me and started talking to me. He introduced himself as Michael and put his arm around me telling me how hot I was. I wiggled out of his embrace and could tell he was intoxicated as he was calling me babe and was asking me what was wrong like he had the right to touch me and we actually knew each other. The bartender actually intercepted and told the guy to leave me alone but the guy would have no part of it. Within seconds, Matt arrives back at my side and was like "*hey babe I am back from the bathroom*", puts his arm around my neck and introduces himself to Michael who immediately backs off and leaves with his tail between his legs thankfully. "*Thank you so much Matt*" I told him and I hugged him hard. "*That guy's a loser and drunk and there is no way I was letting him anywhere near you*" responded Matt. Matt grabbed my hand and we went back over to our seats with Roger returning as well and joined the others to watch the rest of the game, and my cheeks felt flush from Matt's reaction to me being hit on. I wanted him so badly. As the game ended though, we said our goodbyes as friends but I wished for so much more. We got into our Ubers to drive us each home with Roger and I going together back to Bradley Beach. I confided in Roger on the way home that I had a crush on Matt and about how he saved me at the bar from Michael. Roger laughed at me as we drove through the side streets and then arrived finally back at the condos. We said goodbye to the driver and clumsily got out of the elevator, laughing and saying goodnight. Roger told me he didn't think Matt would've have done what he did if he weren't keeping an eye on me too and that made me happy as I closed my door with a smile on my face.

Going forward Roger started hanging out with us more and Jake and the crew actually started really liking Roger, and eventually they even hung out without me around, and he came every Monday night to the bar to see the games. This made me really happy and Roger was a talented artist and an overall nice guy who just needed someone to take a chance on him. Roger and I would often talk well into the night and he spent a lot of time at my condo sharing dinners. He became a great friend and confidante. Roger filled the void of not having Claire near me like before. I never felt alone with Roger living right by me.

A delivery came to my door one evening from Federal Express. I wondered if my father had sent me something as I saw the California address stamped across the top and I couldn't help but smile thinking maybe he missed me after all. I didn't wait to open it and sat on my kitchen chair and quickly ripped the brown paper open. There was a long box and a card inside. I opened the card in anticipation but noticed immediately that it wasn't my father's handwriting but Bennie's cursive but it still made me smile as I remembered he had said he was sending me something. The card read:

Not only because I miss you but because I know how much you love football and you are finally living by your favorite team. Love you Alexandria! Love Always, Bennie

I opened the box and inside were six box seats to the NY Giants game on Saturday night with VIP passes to meet players, and free food and drinks all night long. I literally squealed and instantaneously called Bennie to thank him. I then immediately called Monica to invite her and Robbie. I knew this could be a good opportunity to meet one of my favorite players, Damion Kipson. He was the one player that we hadn't heard back from yet and really wanted him at the autograph signing breakfast we were managing. I needed to convince him to come because he was the fan favorite of so many of the kids. We had made all of the final arrangements for the breakfast and just needed to secure one more big name to make sure tickets sell. The money raised was for the children's hospital and I knew we could use this opportunity to meet players to ask them in person to help. I stopped by Roger's condo and asked him if he wanted to come as well so that just left two spots. I wanted to ask Matt but not necessarily Jake but I knew he would get pissed if I didn't include him and with two spots left, I guess I had no choice so I gave them both a quick call and they quickly accepted. Bennie had arranged for a Black SUV to pick us up and drive us back and forth so that we could drink as much as we wanted without having to drive the hour plus drive to Giants Stadium. I told everyone the tickets were from a friend of my father who worked as an athletic trainer for the NY Giants so that they wouldn't question all of the bells and whistles that came along with VIP tickets and the car service.

Saturday morning arrived and it was the day of the game. The game started at 1:00 p.m. but we had to get there earlier for the meet and greet so everyone arrived at my condo bright and early. I had gotten coffee, bagels and donuts from Dunkin Donuts for everyone and we all wore Giants' jerseys of our favorite players. Jake kept telling me how awesome I was all morning for taking him to the game. I gave everyone a brief tour of my place and Monica and I went out onto the deck for a brief moment because it was chilly and looked out at the ocean. Monica told me she was excited but felt bad about leaving her daughter with her mom again. I realized that I should've included McKenna instead of Jake and I apologized but she stopped me right away and said not to worry. Monica said she just struggled with being a working mom, trying to do some fun things with her husband but also spending quality time with her daughter and as a family. She said McKenna was too young to come and she wouldn't know what was really going on and she would be happier anyway making cookies or doing crafts with Grandma. We re-emerged inside to get out of the cold and I told Monica I would make it up to McKenna and make plans soon to do my butter cookie recipe. Monica told me McKenna had brought it up the other day and was excited.

It was November now and the air was crisp and it was always colder when you were by the ocean. Matt, Jake and Roger sat on stools around the kitchen island eating donuts and drinking coffee and trying to school Roger on football. Despite watching with us on Monday nights, Roger had no idea how the game really worked, however, he must have hit up a sporting goods store as he wore a Giants' Jersey today. He got excited about interceptions not realizing that it's only a good thing when your team is the one making one. Still, Roger had started to like football. I could tell. Not sure if he would admit it, but he was getting into it and coming over to the dark side like me.

This was my first NFL game actually so I couldn't wait myself and texted Bennie that we were on our way as we left our condo and headed to the awaiting SUV. I sat next to Matt in the car and I noticed immediately how good he smelled and I was reminded again that I had a big crush on him. I could only hope he wasn't in a relationship but I wasn't sure. He had never mentioned it and always came alone or with guy friends to our hangouts. I had to find out more about him personally. When we arrived at the stadium, we entered through the VIP entrance with our VIP passes in lanyards around our necks. We were there two hours before the game and got to go out to the bottom of the field and shake hands with various players, take pictures and have them sign footballs and jerseys. Meeting the various players, especially my favorites, and being able to get a picture with each had made my year go from good to great in a matter of minutes. Roger cracked me up as he had players sign footballs and he didn't even know who they were. The moment arrived when Damion Kipson came by and I handed him my business card and told him about the breakfast and asked him to call me. I didn't know if he would, but I had my fingers crossed. He was the player I needed to make this event, my very first at Shore Events, successful. He seemed truly interested but he could've just been trying to be nice so I just had to hope he would follow through.

We then went up to the box seats and there was a buffet of food and two bartenders there. The box had couches and televisions inside and a line of comfy seats to the watch the games in the warm box although being in the stands going crazy seemed like fun too as I saw the face painted fans wrapped in blankets keeping each other warm in each row. Once the game started, there was an immediate interception by the New York Giants defensive player none other than Snacks but otherwise known as Damon Harrison. Snacks had signed a box of Rice Krispy Treats that I brought as a joke and he was an amazing athlete and great guy. He had gotten that nickname of Snacks for his love of exactly that – good ole snacks, especially Rice Krispy Treats. My cheeks hurt from smiling because I was so happy to be watching my favorite team kicking butt.

Roger screamed during the interception and I told him I thought I was in the Twilight Zone and wondered who he was! Roger hugged me and whispered that meeting me this year has been the best thing in his life and I hugged him back. Roger had really come out of his shell but perhaps it was a little alcoholic courage too from the many drinks we had been having. The New York Giants beat the Washington Redskins 27-14 and we had screamed our heads off, ate like pigs and got drunk before heading back to our awaiting SUV to drive us back to Bradley Beach. Bennie always found ways to make me feel special and I smiled as I thought of him and how much I missed him. We talked football the entire way back and despite all of the food we had just devoured in the VIP box, Jake said he was hungry again and we all laughed.

When we got back to my place, we ordered pizza and hung out at my condo. Monica and Robbie left early to go home to McKenna, and Jake finally left after eating pizza because it was now Saturday night and he of course had plans. Roger left for his long walk home down the hall leaving Matt and I alone. Matt told me it was about time that I made plans with him to show him my Skee-Ball skills and we agreed on next weekend. I wasn't sure if he was asking me out or just following through on our bet to challenge one another. I hoped it was more than the challenge. Matt was so easy to talk to. From the moment, I met him there was just something different about him. He was friendly, giving, fun and easy to be around not to mention handsome. I knew he was my co-worker and for all I knew he was involved so I decided to get my courage and to ask him. "*So, Matt, what is your deal? Are you involved with anyone?*" I bravely asked. Matt smiled and answered "*I actually just got out of a relationship. My ex, Linda, and I were high school sweethearts and my mom is friends with her family. So, it's been rough all around because of that fact. My dad was never in the picture so my mother was a single mom who raised me and my brother alone. She never went to college and just worked mainly in waitressing or doing some other odd jobs. There were times we were evicted and lived in our car growing up. Linda's family had helped her out on more than one occasion get back on her feet so we are obviously all very close. My brother is a college student now and my mom is doing great but both families didn't take it well when I broke up with Linda. It's a hard situation but as much as I will always love Linda, there was always something missing. I think it was easy because we have known each other since we were kids but I just knew she wasn't the one if that makes sense.*"

It made total sense to me. I never had found that one person either. Unlike my father's movies full of romance and miracles, I hadn't found the man of my dreams either, although Matt was someone special to me and I didn't even know why. I just knew in my heart somehow and I wondered if maybe I really did experience love at first sight. It was something you heard about and always secretly wanted to experience but never imagined you would. Matt made me feel like a better version of myself just by being around him. Even if Linda wasn't in the picture, they had such a history and that was hard to compete with. Plus, what would Matt want with a girl who grew up in privilege living in mansions and traveling around the world when he had been living in his car as a child. I was afraid to tell him about the real me, although the real me wasn't that girl completely. I grew up without a mother, just as he had grown up without a father. We had more in common than he probably knew. I was lonely most of the time and I didn't have a hard-working single mom that did everything for their kids. I had what I did due to my father's success but also his greed. I would do anything to have a mom or dad that put me first as Matt had in his mother.

"*So what about you Ria? You are beautiful, living on your own, have a great career. Anyone special in your life?*" inquires Matt. "*No. Just wanted to initially focus on getting myself on track doing something I love and then just hope the rest falls into place in that department*" I responded. "*And, what about California? Do you miss it? Or, do you think you'll stay here? Sorry for so many questions. I am just curious*" continued Matt. I answered honestly "*I love California. My father and other important people to me are there but honestly my father travels all the time anyway so it doesn't matter if I am there or here. But I am loving the Jersey Shore. Now I watch sunrises over the ocean instead of sunsets in Los Angeles but I am growing to love it here. I had vacationed here growing up so New Jersey isn't foreign to me. But I mainly like it because it's a family feel in these beach towns and a very similar lifestyle to California, despite the weather of course.*" Matt laughed at that.

It was getting late and Matt said he should head out. He put on his jacket and thanked me for an amazing day. I walked him to my door, and we both paused for a moment saying goodbye. I stared him directly in the eyes hoping he wouldn't spot my desire for him. I wanted him to kiss me but I knew he probably wouldn't. We worked together but he was the one person, besides Monica and Roger who meant something to me. Roger and Monica were terrific friends but Matt was more. I was romantically interested in him but he had just gotten out of a relationship, and I had my life of privilege that I knew wouldn't sit well with him. We look at each other for a brief moment and then I settled for a hug and he went off into the night yelling "*game on for Skee-Ball*" as the elevator doors closed. He lived in Long Branch where our offices were located so he would be home pretty quickly. I cleaned up the pizza and beers and got ready for bed. I texted Claire to check in and see how things were with her in California and filled her in on my big time crush on Matt. I plugged in my phone and as I lay my head on my pillow, I couldn't help but again think of Matt. My mind just couldn't turn him off. He was just so perfect. My phone buzzed and I looked over and saw it was Matt saying good night and sending me a heart emoji and I immediately responded back to him the same and told him how much I liked spending time with him today. I felt like a school girl as I closed my eyes. I just hoped I wasn't setting myself up for a letdown.

At work the following Monday, my phone rang promptly at 9:00 a.m. It was Jessica Lee who introduced herself as Damion Kipson's rep. Damion had agreed to do the breakfast and I took her information to send her the details and contract. I hung up and gave a scream and Matt came running in and I shared the news. Matt gave me a hug and we held each other a little too long when with perfect timing Jordie comes to my office and we pull apart from our embrace. Jordie gives us a sneer and said she was there to do my new hire performance review and check-in. I didn't even know that existed and thought, great, I hope she doesn't want to fire me already. But at least the timing is perfect since I had just booked Damion Kipson for the breakfast. Jordie pushes past Matt as he exits and I wondered if maybe she was perhaps from Hollywood instead of New Jersey with all of her dramatics. Matt made a small gesture at Jordie behind her back to make me laugh and I closed the door trying not die of laughter. Jordie did my review like she was reading a grocery checklist. Dependable – Check. Good Worth Ethic – Check. Pride in Role – Check. Then, in typical Jordie style, she quizzes me on what I have accomplished so far, major successes I would like to share, how I am acclimating to the role and the company and even feedback in general of how the company can do better. I always felt like I was in an interview when I hung around her. I tried to dig a little deeper and ask her some personal things to get to know her as a person when we were wrapped up with my review.

"*So, Jordie, tell me about yourself. Are you from the shore area*?" I inquired. I really was just as curious as probably everyone else in this place because Jordie was so stern, mysterious and almost had an angry feel to her. She was also a workaholic arriving at the crack of dawn and staying till late in the evening. Jordie looked up from her pad and pen and just said "*no, I am not*" and stood up giving me the indication that she obviously didn't want to share. I just said "*ok, well I really do like it here and I've been making great friends in the office and you are welcome to join us if you ever want to for lunch or outside of work. Hope you have a great rest of the day.*" Jordie did crack a small smile and thanked me before she left. It was a tiny breakthrough.

After my review, I got a text from Bennie about Thanksgiving. Thanksgiving is in two weeks and I hadn't even made plans to go home yet and wasn't sure if my father would even be there if I did. I quickly was reminded about that one thing with a lot of Hollywood elite and that is that your career and ego were more important than anything else. While not everyone is like that, a lot of people are and unfortunately my father is so famous and everyone bows down to him so he just lives in his own little world and I wasn't sure if he would grace me with his presence, even if it was a national holiday. But, I knew I would go home and take a chance to see him and also if anything to see Bennie. I responded back to Bennie and told him I would be there and to make the arrangements. I had gotten so caught up in my new life here in New Jersey but I wondered if going home to California would make me homesick. I missed Claire too. We were always together there meeting up for drinks or coffee. I wish I had her closer to me but I knew she was a California girl through and through.

Chapter 5
HOLIDAYS FOR ONE

Jake, Matt, Monica and I had a working lunch on Tuesday to focus on the final touches for this weekend's fast approaching breakfast event. The announcement of special Guest, Damion Kipson, had doubled our ticket sales in one day making this first event a truly successful one before it had even started. But, it also now caused a lot of extra work for us to accommodate for all of the extra guests that were now coming. We were making small talk over lunch and Matt asked me some more questions about my family out in California. I finally got to tell him a little about losing my mother at a young age. I didn't share with him who my father was yet. I wanted him to get to know me better first, and see where things went with him before I broke the news to him on that subject. I knew I had a physical attraction to him but we were still developing our friendship and connection, and just getting to know each other better. Jake chimed in about his upbringing too even though no one had asked him. Jake grew up in a pretty typical middle class household. He was always the star in his family. He was Homecoming and Prom King in High School, super popular, and a Varsity Football and Baseball player, captain on both teams. Things always came easy for him and everyone adored him. He reminded me of my father in a lot of ways because like Jake, my father has everyone worshipping him. Jake never stopped with his flirting though and kept telling me I should be a model, and kept making comments of how beautiful I was. I tried to get him to back off by asking if he saw how small and short I was and that I didn't think modeling agencies would want to hire someone who isn't at least five foot eight inches tall, but Jake continued his flirtatious behavior with me anyway. Finally, Matt interjected and told him to back off. This was the first time I had seen Matt upset but I was glad he seemed to get a bit jealous. Jake didn't expect it either by the look on his face but he did what Matt said.

After our lunch meeting, everyone was back at their desks busy so I decided to give my dad a call and ask him about Thanksgiving. I wasn't sure if he would be free but to my surprise he answered my call and seemed overjoyed to hear from me which melted my heart a little because I really did miss him. Even when I was home in California, he was at least around and even if I just saw him in passing, I knew he was there and could be there for me. We talked for a while this time and he looped me on his latest adventure as an astronaut who saves the world from sheer disaster. I told him about my job and my first football autograph event. He assured me he would be home for Thanksgiving and he would have Bennie book my flights and send me the details. I smiled when I hung up and I decided I finally trusted Roger enough to tell him my secrets. I needed to share it with someone and I was going to tell him tonight. I wanted to tell Matt too but I was still too scared that whatever was happening between us would never get off the ground if he knew. But, I needed someone to confide in. I didn't have Claire here and Roger and I had grown very close.

I invited Roger over that evening and I spent the evening telling Roger about who I really was. I told him how Bennie raised me and was like a second dad. I shared who my mother was, the famous model who had OD'd after getting addicted to pain killers and that I was only a child when I found her on the bathroom floor with foam coming out of her mouth. My mother was best known a famous picture of her holding a margarita with the sun setting in the background and I pointed to her picture hung proudly in my living room and Roger admired it. I told him how I also kept a picture of a sunset in my wallet just to remind me of her. I wished she had lived so that she could've been a bigger part of my life. If she had, I told Roger that my relationship with my father would've been in a very different place as her death spiraled him into focusing on his work more than being home. It made me realize the pain my dad must still be in and the burden he must carry. It must be terribly painful for him and I regretted my anger towards him at that moment.

When I got to who my father was, at first there was excitement from Roger. Roger was a big movie buff and had seen every one of my dad's movies but who hasn't! Roger repeated "Holy crap" a thousand times and couldn't stop saying it but I can't blame him. It's a lot to take in and I told him just imagine being in my shoes and having that reaction every time when people find out, if they don't already know. I made him take an oath and pinky swear this would stay amongst us only. He was never to tell another living person and he promised and I truly believed him. We didn't need Monica, Rachel, Chandler, Ross, Joey and Phoebe – I had my own version of *Friends* right here in this moment and I knew that Roger, Monica and Matt (and maybe Jake HAHA) would always be a part of my life. I told Roger about my feelings for Matt too having grown and how it had gone from a crush to so much more. Roger told me I should give Matt more of a hint that I liked him since Matt obviously wasn't doing that just to see where it got me. I was too shy for that surprisingly. I had never been shy before with men, but I didn't want to mess anything up with Matt. I told Roger that I wasn't ready yet to share about my father with him because Matt had such a hard and poor life growing up, and I was afraid he would hold my wealth against me. I knew I had to tell him eventually but I wasn't going to anytime soon. Roger told me it was probably for the best to keep it between us for now but I would have to be honest eventually or it would make it worse. He knew Monica would be fine with it and probably Matt too but he wasn't so sure about Jake. I agreed and I couldn't help but think about how Jake judged Roger when he first started hanging out with us. Roger said in good time, I will know the right moment to tell Matt and I hoped he was right. He also said I shouldn't wait too long or Matt will not like if I started out something with him with lies. I just hoped Matt could accept my background and not wonder if I am spoiled and privileged, and be able to agree that we were exact opposites in the way we were raised but it didn't matter.

Matt and I were so busy with the breakfast that we had to put our Skee-Ball plans on hold until after the event was over and Thanksgiving was done. But now, it was finally the day of the breakfast and as promised Damion Kipson arrived along with a few other Giants' players for the breakfast. They were all on time and we had arranged for them to eat as well at first away from the rest of the guests in a separate room. I was tasked with bringing them food and re-filling their coffee. I had to assess when they looked like they were getting full, and then we would pull them to a special room with a long table and people could come up at their convenience or form small lines to meet them and they could bring an item or two to have them sign it. Once they were in the room and ready for our guests, we announced to the excited crowd they could start lining up. The players were really gracious, and they all signed autographs for our guests and spent a lot of time talking with each person. We also had them sign extra shirts and balls to deliver later at the children's hospital along with donating the check from funds and contributions raised from the event that we would present to them.

Everyone from our office was there at this breakfast except for the CEO and Managing Director who were traveling. Even Jordie was here. She didn't normally participate in events since her role was more in the office but she was there kind of helping out by herself. She never even approached any of the players either for autographs so I wondered why she had even come. Jordie kept hanging out with Matt and it appeared like she was flirting with him. Her robotic style was suddenly a little less so but still a little stiff as she will never be completely loose. But, she seemed to also be comfortable around Matt and maybe like me, he too brought out the best in her. When Jordie wasn't looking though, Matt rolled his eyes at me and I laughed. Maybe he didn't want me to think he liked her. I still couldn't quite figure her out. I had threw her a bone to be friends but she didn't seem receptive. But, I guess she did show up today. I knew she too definitely had a crush on Matt. But at least Matt seemed to have zero interest.

Later in the afternoon, Matt and I volunteered to be the ones to go over to the hospital so that we could do the task of handing out the signed memorabilia and presenting the hospital administration with a check for $10,000 to the hospital. Matt and I were elated. Never in my life had I felt like I was making a difference more than I did in this moment. I loved this job and what I could do for the community. Although being at the breakfast and around the players of my favorite football team was super amazing, the thing that made me happiest was this moment now seeing the smiles on the faces of these kids as we walked around the rooms and handed out signed items to special patients. Matt and I spent a lot of time in a young patient's room who was suffering from a life threatening heart condition. His name was Billy and he had a love for Superman. My dad had played Superman in a series of movies with the most recent one out just last year. Billy was obsessed with Superman and my father. He had a signed picture of my father next to his bed, but I could tell it wasn't real and not my father's handwriting but it made him happy and that's all that mattered. Billy and his struggles left a permanent mark on my heart. He was the reason this job was so important to me. We had made his day stopping by with gifts from the New York Giants. My heart was full and my eyes full of tears. We were giving back and I felt completely elated to be standing here in this moment making a difference even if it was a small one in the obstacles these kids have ahead of them. I wish my father could've seen this moment and his picture next to a patient's bed. It would be the perfect way to remind him how important he is to so many people and he should embrace his celebrity for good deeds and not selfish rewards.

Both Matt and I turned to leave Billy's room and looked at each other with smiles on our faces. As we finished our last room and entered back into the hallway, I just grabbed Matt and gave him a long, hard hug. Matt ran his fingers through my hair as we embraced and he didn't even need to ask me what that the hug was for. We both knew how this made us feel and I think for the first time, we both realized how being around each other made us feel too. He kept me in his embrace as he turned to face me and pressed his forehead against mine and squeezed me tighter before we parted. He still had his hands in mine and we just smiled at each other and hugged one more time. I held onto Matt's arm as we walked to the elevator together and we just kept talking about the day and how it made us each feel.

Matt and I were walking to our cars making plans to go out and celebrate. He grabbed my hand as we walked and I felt like a schoolgirl. I couldn't wait to see where tonight would take us. Matt was mentioning Surf Taco and some other restaurants that he enjoyed and he said he wanted to take me to all of them as we walked through the dimly lit parking lot. I was about to answer him when I noticed a woman waiting for him by his car. "*It's Linda…ugh*" whispered Matt to me. "*It's o.k. We can do it another time*" I told him but inside I was crushed and disappointed. There was finally progress and then this happens and we slowly released holding hands to avoid the already awkward moment. Whenever Matt and I had a chance to finally be alone and explore what was happening between us, there was always someone in the way. Linda was my biggest fear though. They had a history and one that was close to Matt's heart. Matt introduced me and asked Linda what she was doing there as I got into my car and waved goodbye. I looked back at them in my rearview mirror and could tell Linda looked upset and was pleading with him to talk to her. My heart broke for Linda but I wanted Matt's heart too. I felt helpless as I drove away. I wanted to turn around so badly but I knew I needed to let them talk and whatever was meant to be would be.

Despite this low, it had been a good day. I was leaving this week to go home for Thanksgiving and we had meetings on Monday with our next big project assignment. I was excited for a new focus to make a difference somewhere. But, even with all of these things to keep my mind busy, my heart wasn't doing so good. In fact, it currently sat in the pit of my stomach over Matt. When I arrived home, I skipped dinner and could do nothing but think about what may have happened between Matt and Linda and if they went somewhere to talk and get back together. I always thought the worst but I think we all do when we can't control what's happening around us. I tried to remember to leverage my positivity but it wasn't working. I wondered if Matt would bring up Linda to me on Monday or if he wouldn't say a word. I was dying inside to know what happened. He held my hand on his own so I felt like he was giving me signals that he liked me finally. I hoped that I wouldn't lose him to Linda but at the same time, if he was still in love with her, than I had to move on and accept it.

Monday morning, we were back at work and had a meeting first thing. Matt walked into the conference room bringing in these amazing donuts from a small shop in Allenhurst, NJ called "Broad Street Donuts". They had these flavors and creations that I had never seen at your traditional donut shop. I had mentioned to Matt a few weeks ago that I had driven by this place a few times and wanted to stop in. I hoped he had gone there for me but I also hoped it wasn't out of guilt for getting back with Linda and breaking my heart. Matt winked at me and sat right next to me as we learned of our next team assignment. “These look awesome” I said to Matt referring to the donuts. “I knew you wanted to try them so I stopped there on my way in to the office” Matt whispered smiling. The knots in my stomach started to feel better but only slightly as I still had Linda in the back of my mind. I grabbed a donut called “the boardwalk” which was vanilla with tons of rainbow sprinkles and tried to brighten my mood.

Monica started the meeting and advised us of our new project. The assignment was called Secret Celebrity Santa. We had to convince celebrities or well-known locals to become Secret Santa’s for deserving people who had displayed kindness or showcased having a financial need in the community and only had a few weeks to pull this off. This assignment hit home with me because I knew if I would just tell them who my father is, I could probably have every connection in the world to make this event the biggest and best it could ever be. I didn’t want to use my contacts and network. I wanted to just be able to find willing participants just for being me. And, I wasn’t sure if I should let the cat out of the bag yet so I signed up to focus on finding the needy families and people in the community who had done good deeds that I could nominate as the recipients, while Matt and Jake were handling celebrity involvement and Monica handling the gifts and media component. This was such an amazing thing but it also gave me anxiety. I was glad it was finally almost Thanksgiving and I could get a break from this assignment and to keep my mind off Matt, if that was possible. He never did tell me what happened with Linda, not that he had to but I had hoped he would.

It was the Wednesday before Thanksgiving in the office. Everyone had pretty much headed out but I was one of the last to go. Most people in my office would probably stay local so they had hit the road early to head home and spend time with their families. But, I had to fly and my private plane wasn’t going till the evening since it was an overnight flight. I had my head down towards my phone as I walked down the hall to grab a late afternoon coffee before I would head out when I crashed right into Matt. "*Sorry Matt. I thought I was the only one here still*" I told him. Matt ran his fingers through his blonde hair and seemed nervous. I couldn't help but look into his blue eyes and think 'we are finally alone.'

"Oh my God, I am so sorry Ria" said Matt. "*It's not your fault, it's me. I can't text and walk apparently"* I replied laughing and smiling. "*I am about to head out but I hope you have a nice Thanksgiving Matt."* I wanted so badly to ask him what had happened with Linda the other night but I was too afraid to hear his answer. *"You too Ria and are we still on for Skee-Ball? And, again sorry about the other night"* he rambled. *"I had no idea Linda would show up. She won't leave me alone or get the hint. I feel bad but I just don't feel the same way so it's been difficult for her to accept."* I took a deep breath and answered feeling relieved *"It's not a big deal Matt. But, I was looking forward to hanging out so let's make our Skee-Ball Plans for when I return so we finally can"* he agreed and I hugged him goodbye and he wished me a Happy Thanksgiving and safe travels. I was happy as I was locking up my office taking my coffee to go that he had brought up Linda on his own and it sounded like they were not back together. I was even happier though that he remembered about Skee-Ball and made sure to remind me. I couldn't wait to hang out with him alone and see where it took us.

I left the office and returned to my home. I had just finished packing my bag and was just grabbing a glass of water in the kitchen when Bennie texted me that the car service was waiting so I hurried back to my bedroom and grabbed my suitcase and headed out riding the elevator with Roger. Roger was going to his parent's house for Thanksgiving in Northern New Jersey. Like me, he was an only child. Roger gave me a hug as I hopped into the car service and I was on my way. As I sat in the backseat, my thoughts began drifting to Matt again. Matt texted me calling me crash for bumping into him earlier and wishing me a good weekend as the car service drove to the airport. I couldn't help but think about if Matt would see Linda over the weekend but in our text conversation he said he was going to his mom's apartment and spending time with his mom and brother and he was already craving his mom's stuffing. So, I was hopeful. He seemed like he had a nice family and Matt seemed like a great guy. There was something about him that just drew me in and drove me crazy. I finally arrived at the airport and was on my way to sunny California. A part of me missed California tremendously and I was glad to be going home.

We took off on time luckily. I sunk into my seat and fell fast asleep. I didn't even wake up until the pilot announced we were making our way into the Los Angeles area. When I landed in California, Bennie awaited me giving me the biggest hug ever as I exited the plane. We had both missed each other so much and I really was happy to be home. I handed Bennie a signed football from Damon "Snacks" Harrison, his favorite player, and he was thrilled. Bennie drove me home and asked me a million questions although he already knew everything happening with me as he has texted me every day from the day I had arrived in New Jersey. Funny how I had talked to my real father only twice and yet Bennie found the time to check in with me almost every day. Since I had flew a red eye, it was early on Thanksgiving morning when I arrived at my home. As soon as the door opened, I could smell turkey cooking and the sounds of clutter and chaos coming from the kitchen staff, despite the early hours. Bennie headed to check on them in the kitchen while I made my way up the stairs to my room to drop off my suitcase feeling like a child again, and then tiptoeing down the hall to my father's bedroom. I slowly opened the door and when I looked in, I saw my father fast asleep with some stranger next to him. It was a woman that looked around my age to be honest and I kind of just smirked and went back to my room to soak in being home. I lay on my bed and looked around my room and felt comfortable like I never had left, but a part of me was missing my condo in New Jersey for some reason. I felt like a child here I guess and not the adult I had become.

My father finally poked his head in around noon with no sign of the woman so I didn't even mention it. He gave me a hug and I melted into his arms. He may be one of the most famous men in the world, but to me, he is just simply my father. I took a shower and put on a pink sundress, my favorite color, and at around 4:00 p.m., we had our Thanksgiving dinner outside by the pool. It was my dad, myself, Bennie and a few other staff members along with another famous couple – Tom Bennett and his wife Nancy, who also worked in the business, but had no children. I was just happy my dad was there and he seemed happy. Bennie never married and didn't seem to have much family. He mainly just spent his whole life with us and he had become part of our family. I smiled at Bennie and then brought my eyes back to my father. I couldn't help but notice his eyes seemed a little tighter and he was probably now getting Botox to keep up his youthful looks. It felt so good to be home but I also just wished I would have some alone time with just my father but there were always people over taking up his time and talking business. I was glad that woman from his bed earlier this morning was not a guest at our meal too.

Tom and Nancy shifted their conversation from my father to me and asked when I was going to enter the business, and I told them I wasn't sure and just wanted to enjoy being a normal person for a while. Tom looked at me shamefully like I was disappointing the world. I told them about my job and the kind of work we were doing. Tom and Nancy told me it was wonderful but that I should look in the mirror and know how many people would die to be me with my beauty. Tom was all about the world of show business but I could tell Nancy didn't really care and wanted me to be happy. Nancy told me I was bred with the looks needed to make it in this business and she put her arm around me and told me I was going to break a lot of hearts in New Jersey. That comment was her way of telling me that she was o.k. with whatever I did. She came up with me to my bedroom after our meal and brushed my hair and did my make-up like I was twelve years old. I had been without a motherly figure since a child so I guess it felt good to feel that bonding moment in a way. I liked the nurturing I got from her and I let her do it. She told me I was perfection and beauty like my mom. Nancy had modeled with my mom when she was younger so I had known her my whole life. The thing with Hollywood is I didn't know if she meant it or if she just was telling me what I wanted to hear. But, I knew Nancy probably meant it. It felt good to have a woman's maternal touch for a brief moment. I hoped that one day when I got married and had a mother-in-law that I would have a close relationship with her. I had been without a mother for so long and I missed mine terribly.

After the guests left, my dad, Bennie and I hung out watching television and I asked them what we were going to do this weekend, but my dad said he was only around in the morning tomorrow and then flying out to do scenes for the astronaut movie in Cape Canaveral, Florida where the space shuttle was. I lay my head on his shoulder as we watched television and just tried to enjoy the moment because I knew it would be short-lived. I had breakfast with my father the next morning before he left and then Bennie and I spent the rest of the weekend together going to arcades, shopping and eating at our favorite places. My manicurist came to my house for a manicure and pedicure and I invited Claire to join me. We both enjoyed a manicure and pedicure and used this time together to catch up. I looped her in on Matt and she was excited for me. I told her I was hoping our Skee-Ball adventure would be the one to push us past the friend zone. She told me to keep her posted and I told her she needed to come visit me soon, but may be best to wait until the weather is a little nicer and we could go to a movie night at *The Asbury* and enjoy the beach.

After Claire left, I saw a group of friends from high school Saturday for about an hour for a drink as well before I took the red eye back to Newark, New Jersey for an early arrival on Sunday. The long weekend felt short when you spend half of it in an airplane but it was worth the flying time to see Bennie and spend time with my dad and my friends. The group I was with from high school were all socially elite and working in the business. I was included because of who I was but they had all chosen the path of fame and were well on their way to achieving it too. I had known all of them since elementary school so I always saw them at least a few times each year to keep in touch but ultimately, I had nothing in common with them anymore, except childhood memories. I had one drink and got caught up in their world of glitz and glamour while answering questions about what movies my dad was working on now. Luckily, I could keep my visit short as I had to leave and grab my bag and have Bennie take me back to the airport and be on my way back to the Garden State, as New Jersey is often called. And before you knew it, my weekend in California was over and I was on my way back to New Jersey, and to Matt.

It was cold arriving back in New Jersey after being home in the warmth of California and Los Angeles' never-ending sunshine but it felt good to be back. It was like coming home to my independence again and away from the shelter of my father. When I arrived back, the condo complex was quiet as many people were still not back from their travels so I settled back home, going through my mail and making my Christmas list. Our holiday party at work was coming up and we each brought a generic gift for a lucky co-worker and placed it under the tree and you would just pick one to take home and have a surprise. We were also asked to bring a donation of a toy for local needy families. I was happy and excited to do the gift donation for the needy family but other than a gift card, I was at a loss on what generic gift to put under the tree for a member of our team to grab. I made a cup of coffee for myself and tried to brainstorm some ideas of what the heck I could buy. About half way through my coffee, it came to me and I decided to get a gift certificate from a local restaurant to support local or small businesses and keep up the theme of what Shore Events stood for - community. I was getting the hang of this job and I appreciated how much Shore Events and this job meant to me.

I figured I'd get a head start on work and I started to do some research on the internet for our project on stories from the area of people that had done an act of kindness or for resources locally that could help identify needy families that could use a Secret Santa in their corner. Matt texted me asking if I made it back safely and asked me about my weekend. I told him about spending time with my father but left out the movie stars at my house for Thanksgiving, and them trying to get me to get into the business part but I did tell him about Bennie, calling him my Uncle and the fun things we did. I asked him about his mom's stuffing and told him if he had leftovers, I wanted to try some. For a few days, I had distanced my thoughts from Matt. I tried to just be in the moment and cherish my time in California with family and friends. I knew one thing for sure…I needed to figure out what was happenings between us or it was going to drive me crazy.

Monica called me as well and mentioned going to the bar for Monday Night Football tomorrow since we had missed a few being so busy with the other event and I told her yes. Monica, Robbie and McKenna had hosted Thanksgiving and she told me it was fun but she is exhausted, and glad it was over but ultimately just happy she didn't burn the turkey. I walked down the hall and knocked on Roger's door and told him about my weekend as well and reminded him about Monday Night Football. He told me that he planned on coming to the bar tomorrow night after work too. Roger invited me in for a bit and showed me his latest art piece. He had drawn a decorative and detailed portrait of a woman who had fallen asleep on a bench. She was in black and white yet all that was around her was detailed and colorful full of bright flowers and elaborate, beautiful scenery. When Roger was explaining his portrait, he told me it represented the way people missed life happening around them. His art really did imitate life for so many people. We all forget to look around once in a while, smell the roses as they say, or just appreciate the beauty in the world. I knew I would never look the same way at Roger. He was truly just incredible. And, he was so right. If you don't stop to look, you will never see the beauty all around us, or even within ourselves. It reminded me of myself and my desire to blend in. Maybe blending in didn't mean hiding and not being myself after all. Maybe I wasn't really looking to blend in but rather to find myself, gain acceptance and my happiness. Perhaps I wasn't running from the possibility of fame but from just wanting to find someone or something genuine in my life.

After work on Monday, we all met up at the bar for Monday Night Football. This time the New England Patriots were playing the Miami Dolphins. The New England Patriots had an amazing franchise and winning history. I knew everyone called Tom Brady the GOAT when he played for them but I was secretly hoping for a Dolphins win as I had carried a torch for former quarterback, Dan Marino, back in the day. Matt walked in and he looked more handsome than ever. He wore simple jeans and a long sleeved t-shirt but I liked seeing him casual since we were always so dressed up for work. Jake, Matt, Roger, Monica, Robbie and I sat at large round table watching the game and catching up on our Thanksgiving weekend, talking a little about work, and reminiscing about being at the New York Giant's game. It was back to our routine and I loved this tradition we were creating.

As we were all hanging out and watching the game, I got a tap on my shoulder. I turned and saw it was my old flame from my Spring Lake days, Mercer. As excited as I was to see him, my heart raced a little too because Matt was sitting right next to me and I was afraid he would find out now about my father from overhearing something from Mercer. I excused myself from the table and Roger kept everyone busy telling stories so that the focus wouldn't be on me as he knew Mercer knew who I really was by the look on my face. I could see Matt watching out of the corner of my eye as I talked to Mercer. "*I can't believe you are here Alexandria*" said Mercer giving me a hug. "*When did you move to New Jersey and how is 'Alexander the Great' doing*?" he asked, referring to my father. "*I know. I don't think I have your number anymore and I have been so busy with work. These are actually my work colleagues and we do special events locally. I am living over in Bradley Beach right now. As for my father, he is still doing his thing if you know what I mean. It's so good to see you. What are you up to*?" I replied. This was my worst nightmare because I didn't want my friends to find out like this so I just hoped Mercer would talk to me and then rejoin his friends and not come sit with us the entire time after we spoke. Mercer filled me in that he is still in school. He was in med school at Fordham University but just home for the long weekend and was heading back to the Bronx tomorrow where the school is located. I kind of breathed a sigh of relief knowing he wouldn't be around too much. After a few minutes, I told Mercer I should return to my friends but we should exchange numbers now that I am in the area so we did. As I walked back to the table, Mercer yelled "*tell your father the astronaut, mobster, FBI agent, alien that I said hello*" and I laughed. I could see Matt's confusion by Mercer's comment but Roger kept on story-telling and I nudged him a thank you under the table for saving my ass.

Chapter 6
BELIEVING IN FATE

This busy week was getting busier. After Monday Night Football with my colleagues and friends, running into Mercer, and tomorrow was already my holiday party at work, you would think I would have a simple office day on Tuesday ensuring that I ,stay in Tuesday evening for a quiet night at home. But, I had something else in mind. In doing my exploration for Secret Celebrity Santa, I was inspired by the acts of kindness I had seen. Whether it was paying off layaways, or picking up the tab for the car behind you at a drive-through to pay it forward, there were people everywhere making a difference, even in a small way. On my way into the office I went through a Dunkin Donuts drive-thru to grab breakfast. In the spirit of the season, I paid for the car behind me and left to head out on my way to the office. It was actually exhilarating as I pulled away leaving the person left to wonder as to who paid for them. On my lunch break from work, I let the team know I had to run an errand and instead, I ran over to the Children's Hospital. I met with the administration there to learn about any hardships of medical expenses that families were facing.

"*Is this for the Secret Celebrity Santa project*?" asked Lynne, the Chief Executive Officer of Administration at the hospital. "*Actually Lynne, it's not. We are still doing that of course too but this has nothing to do with Shore Events. I want to do something special myself this holiday season and would like to help a family in need personally. I guess you could say*

I want to be a Secret Santa too" I smiled. "*That's amazing Ria that you want to do something so special for someone.*" Lynne stopped to think for a moment and then continued. "*We do have a unique situation with a boy who has a sudden diagnosis of Osteosarcoma. This is a very rare bone cancer that is often fatal. He has a long battle ahead of him and I know his parents are going to be at least $100,000 in debt when it's said and done, and that's if he even makes it through. They were trying to set up a GoFundMe page to help drive donations because they are already struggling knowing the kind of care their son is going to need to make it through this sickness. If you want to make a donation, I can find out if the GoFundMe page is set up or find out more about the family and then I'll email or text you but that is one that immediately comes to mind.*" I thanked Lynne and asked her not to share our conversation with anyone but thanked her for her guidance. "*God bless you Ria for putting others first*" Lynne stated as I left her office and I thanked her and headed back to work.

I went back to my office but made a quick stop in the lobby at the café to grab a coffee to bring back to my desk as I knew there was a lot of work to do and tomorrow would be a shorter day given the early release for our holiday party. I waited on a short line for my coffee and started to think about the boy Lynne and I discussed and it sounded like the perfect scenario for me to help out his family. I placed my order and paid when I suddenly got a tap on my shoulder as I was sliding my credit card back into my wallet. I turned around to see Matt standing two people behind me and I smiled and said hello. He was also grabbing a coffee and he asked if I wanted to come with him on an errand and I gladly agreed, despite all of the work I had to do. I was never the sit at a desk all day type so I would take any excuse to get out again for a bit. "*The only thing is the errand isn't local*" shared Matt once he finally paid and joined me to wait for his coffee. "*One of the Secret Santa gifts has come in and I need to go into Midtown/New York City and pick it up.*

Apparently though, it weighs less than ten pounds so assuming we will have no problem carrying it and getting it back here if we just go by train. I really hate driving into the city with the traffic and would much prefer the train" Matt finished. "*I would love to join you Matt. I don't think I have it in me to stare at my computer screen the rest of the day*" I answered. We left Shore Events offices and we headed over to the train station with our coffees in our hands and took the 1:35 p.m. train to New York City. There was literally no one on the train at this time of day so we enjoyed the ride, and the quiet. "*Why do we have to go pick this gift up in person? They couldn't just send it by messenger*? I asked not only to make conversation but because I really did think it was strange to require in person delivery. "*And what is the gift*?" I included in my questioning because it must be something good for all this trouble. "*Wish I knew*" responded Matt.

The train ride took about 1 ½ hours since most trains from the Jersey Shore into New York City are local, and make tons of stops. It was already around 3:30 p.m. by the time we made it to our destination in Midtown Manhattan. We went to the heart of Times Square and entered into the lobby of the Knickerbocker Hotel and took the elevator up to their rooftop bar area, only staying on the inside portion since it was much too cold to have the outdoor space operational today. We were met there by Emily, the assistant of New York Yankees pitcher, Brett Stevens. Brett was a Secret Celebrity Santa for a family of four in Neptune, New Jersey who had lost everything in a fire. They were in a new home now but still had very little. Their children were both in elementary school, and they were struggling to make ends meet. They barely had any furniture still, very little clothing, and although no one was home at the time of the fire that took their home, they unfortunately lost their family dog in the blaze, which was probably what broke their hearts the most. Brett had agreed to a $20,000 donation to the family to get back on their feet as well as a gift. Emily greeted us and I almost felt like I was doing something illegal or shady meeting in the dark corner of a bar in the middle of Manhattan to do our exchange, and I held onto Matt as we approached her and he whispered to me "*I know. I feel shady and kind of scared too*." God, I loved this man.

"*Hi, I am Emily and work with Mr. Stevens. Thank you for meeting with me and here is the envelope with the donation and I also have the special gift in a basket over here*" Emily shared cheerfully as she reached for the basket and handed it to me after giving the envelope to Matt. I looked inside the basket and noticed blankets with a small little head sticking out of a fast asleep tiny Yorkie puppy. My face lit up brighter than every light in Manhattan with complete thrill when I saw this adorable little sweetheart cuddled in the blankets and I wanted to just snuggle him into my chest but didn't want to disturb him either. Emily smiled and said "*You have no idea how hard it is for me to turn him over to you. Mr. Stevens knew the family had lost their dog in the fire and thought a new puppy may bring them joy. I am afraid you'll be stuck watching him for a little while until you do your reveal but it was the only time I could get him to you*." I smiled and told her "*This is so amazing Emily. I think between Matt and I we will probably fight over who is going to watch him and I just hope we have the heart to even give him away. He is adorable*."

Emily left and Matt and I decided to hurry back to the train to try and catch the 4:30p train back to Long Branch, New Jersey on NJ Transit because we wanted to try and beat as much of the mad rush as possible given the fact that we now had a very special little passenger with us. Since we had this little guy, we decided to take the subway down to NY Penn Station so that he wasn't out in the cold too long. We made it through the subway and into NY Penn Station to the waiting area to see which gate we would have to run to once it was shown so that we could safely get this puppy onto the train and ensure we had seats next to each other. Matt told me that he was hoping to hang out and grab a drink and spend a little time while we are in New York City but that kind of got thrown out once the puppy came into the picture. A few minutes past as we stood waiting to see our track, yet the puppy was still fast asleep despite all of the noises of NY Penn Station, and finally Gate 1 appeared and Matt and I quickly ran to that escalator and onto the train securing a two-seater together. "*I've got to tell you. It's going to be really hard for me to give this cutie up. I can't wait for him to wake up so that I can kiss him and hold him. I've wanted a dog my entire life. We never could have one because we were mainly in apartments and they didn't allow it. And, now, still, I am in an apartment with a no pet policy so I hate to say this, but I think you will have to take him and my heart is just a little broken because of it*" said Matt frowning. "*YES*!!" I yelled because I was definitely wanting this little guy for a few days. I knew Roger could watch him for me too while I was at work and I could corner him off in my kitchen so that he didn't go to the bathroom all over my house. There was about a half an hour left on the train ride when the little puppy awoke with a squeaky yawn. I nudged Matt and told him "*He's up Matt! You can lift him up first since I know I'll get more time with him*" and that made Matt smile as he reached into the basket and scooped him up into his arms.

The puppy gave soft kisses to Matt and he joked with me that he couldn't wait to tell his brother that he was on the train with Ria and he got some tongue. We both laughed pretty hard at that one. The puppy was suddenly full of energy, biting the snaps on Matt's jacket and climbing from my lap to Matt's and back again. I suddenly wondered if we could even have a dog on the train but we were pulling into Long Branch, New Jersey now anyway and we ran to Matt's truck and sat there waiting to warm up and playing with our new friend until his heat kicked in. I asked Matt if he wanted to come over for dinner and order Chinese food or something so that he could hang out with the puppy for a little while and

Matt answered yes before I could even finish the sentence. I was glad Matt loved dogs because in my mind, that was a requirement if you wanted to be around me. Matt drove me back to the office to retrieve my car and I let him ride with the puppy to my place since my car was still cold and I didn't want the poor little guy to get sick.

We pulled into my complex and parked and carried the puppy in his basket into my place being careful like we were bringing home a newborn baby. Matt and I ordered Chinese and played with the puppy until the delivery man arrived. My house was definitely not puppy proof so Matt and I found one of my cardboard boxes from my move and we made a makeshift wall to keep him in the kitchen so that he would have a place to stay while I was at work, and so that we could eat in peace for a minute too. We shared some Lo Mein and Sesame Chicken and poured two glasses of red wine. Matt and I talked about the puppy and wanting dogs someday too. Matt said he didn't care what type but he wanted to get two maybe one from a breeder and one rescue dog. All of the puppy talk made me think about the fact that Emily had just given us this puppy with no dog food or anything so Matt and I searched the basket but luckily found a small bag of food, his paperwork and shot information as well as some written instructions, and of course some small toys and bones. The last thing I felt like doing was running to store to buy stuff so I was happy about that. I took some comfortable blankets and folded them into a corner of my kitchen for him to sleep on, although I had a strong feeling he was going to rip them to shreds.

Matt's brother facetimed him and Matt answered and said "*I have some news. You know that girl Ria I told you about?*" Matt's brother Ryan answered "*the hot one from California?*" and Matt blushed and told him to shut up under his breath. "*Yes, well we both got some tongue today on the train from Manhattan*" to which his brother started to respond *"you dog!"* but *Matt* quickly turned the camera to me holding this wiggly puppy who was kissing my face. "*Awwww, you guys got a puppy together already*?" Ryan asked to which Matt embarrassingly said "*let me call you later*." Matt continued to look slightly embarrassed and red in the face. Shortly after, he said he better head home as it was getting late and I told him I had a feeling I was going to be sleeping on the kitchen floor and if I don't show up tomorrow, he knows where to find me. Matt laughed and gave me a quick hug and then hit the road. After Matt left for the night, I texted Roger to come over real quick to meet my house guest and he agreed that he would watch him for me while I was at my holiday party tomorrow, and I could just pick him up the following day so that I didn't have to worry about him. I made 100% sure because having a puppy all day tomorrow and then all night was going to be a lot but Roger cradled him like a baby and I could tell Roger didn't mind one bit. I gave Roger the spare copy of my key and he said he would come in the morning after I leave for work to get his house guest, and told me he had a crate still from his family dog that he could use if the guy gets too crazy.

Roger left and the puppy had peed all over my floor so I cleaned it up, and then played with him and I could tell he was ready to crash again. I guess just like a baby, puppies sleep all the time. I wanted to name him so badly but I knew if I did, it would make me more attached. I lay him on the soft blankets and dimmed the light and snuck out to quickly go to bed because I knew it wouldn't be long before I heard whimpering to come and get him and I would be just the sucker to cave in and do it. At 1:00 a.m., my little friend made himself known. I got up, running down my stairs and scooped him up ignoring the pee all over the floor and brought him into my bed building a wall of pillows so he wouldn't fall off. To my surprise, he lay right on my chest and fell back asleep. I think he liked to listen to my heartbeat and it probably made him feel safe. I woke up at 4:00 a.m. to puppy kisses in my ear, nose and mouth. I couldn't think of cuter guy to be waking up to and I decided to just get up for the day since I could tell, he wasn't going back to sleep any time soon like he did earlier.

I brought him into the kitchen and gave him some food and water to which he started eating happily so I quickly cleaned up the pee from the night before and then hopped in the shower to get ready for work. I did my makeup in the kitchen to keep him company and then carried him with me to my closet while I figured out what I was going to wear to the holiday party today. I knew we were casual and going bowling so I just put on cute jeans and a shirt, and made sure I brought socks with me for the bowling shoes. I unplugged my phone and noticed a text from the night before that I had missed with all the excitement of this puppy. It was from Lynne at the Children's Hospital. She sent me the link to the family's GoFundMe page that she had been telling me about. They only had $375 of their $100,000 goal. I pulled out my Red American Express card and charged $99,625 to pay off their upcoming medical expenses for their son, anonymously of course, and then texted Lynne back to thank her. I only wish I could be there when they log on to check their page and see that they had reached their goal. I have never felt so good in my life, except I wished I could stay home all day and play with this puppy who isn't even mine. I can't even imagine when I get my own dog, or worse when I have kids. I am never going to be able to leave them! I knew now how hard it was for Monica to leave her daughter every day.

I kissed my little friend goodbye knowing he would be safe with Roger until tomorrow. He gave me soft kisses and I took in the smell of his puppy breath and gave him a squeeze before giving him a small bone to chew on to keep him busy for a little while. I snapped a quick photo of him and texted it to Matt saying "good morning from your little friend" and a dog emoji with a heart. I walked out to the elevator and walked on. Just as the door was shutting, I could see Roger already heading towards my apartment in a rush and it made me chuckle. He must have been up early waiting for me to leave. I wasn't sure who likes puppies more, me, Matt or Roger! I walked out to my car and hopped in and then let it warm up for a bit before heading to Starbucks. We had our café at work but I really needed strong coffee this morning after only a few hours of sleep. Matt texted me back as I drove through the Starbucks drive-through and said he missed him and I told him Roger was watching him until tomorrow for me. I pulled into the office, coffee in hand, and got to my desk to start my day. I texted Bennie real quick to tell him what I had done for this boy at the Children's Hospital. Bennie told me he wouldn't have expected anything else from me. He said I should do something every December to celebrate the holiday season and to give back. I couldn't think of a better tradition to start and agreed that I would. Between spending time with Matt, hanging out with an adorable puppy and having the opportunity to help a family in need, my heart was feeling full and I was in one of the happiest moods I had been in for a while.

Jordie had popped into my office again asking about the puppy and telling me that Matt had told her all about him. I found it weird being so early in the morning and Matt had just gotten here and it made me wonder if they did speak outside of work. So, now I had Linda AND Jordie possibly to worry about. I filled her in on the cuteness, showing her pictures and that my friend was watching him today and tonight for me. Jordie got a text and then abruptly left per usual. I decided to stop by and quickly see Matt so I poked my head into Matt's office and told him that Jordie asked about the puppy. Matt told me confidentially that Jordie's sister is the one who lost their house in the house fire so she knew about the Secret Santa gifts and was the one who I guess helped make suggestions on what would make them happy. Matt also told me that he had walked in at the same time as Jordie this morning and that's how she knew about the puppy's arrival and I gave a sigh of relief. "*What is Jordie's deal, Matt?*" I asked. "*Jordie and her sister grew up in the*

Boston area I believe" shared Matt. *"Their parents have passed away already and her sister had moved to Neptune, NJ because her husband got a job in the area so Jordie followed to be near her and found a job at Shore Events a few months before you got here. I was the one who on-boarded her since we didn't have a human resources person and she was the one taking that role so I feel like she has a little bit of an affinity to me because I helped her transition into the company. And when the fire happened, she had to take some time off and I helped her out by doing some stuff for her here at work and organizing donations."* I responded *"Oh, that makes sense and sorry to hear about her loss*." Matt finished and said "*Jordie is the one who helped her sister get back on her feet but I think she put herself in some debt too because of that and works like a dog because of it to make sure her job is secure here but as you can tell, she over does it*." We both laughed a little but at least Jordie now made sense to me a little more. I could also see where she had some trust in Matt. It wasn't necessarily a crush after all.

Chapter 7
NEW ASSIGNMENT/NEW BEGINNING

Wednesday night was an early holiday party at work. We had way too much work with the Secret Celebrity Santa project to have it too close to Christmas but I was excited. I had purchased my local restaurant gift card and placed it under the tree for someone to grab and placed my donated toy in the designated area before heading to the lobby to car pool over to our party. It was just a bowling party with terrible food but we were all looking forward to it as well as getting out of the office for a while. Matt quickly comes up to me to warn me about his amazing bowling skills to which I challenged him to prove and we decided upon a bet if someone scores better than the other the most games. Despite my Skee-Ball talents, the truth is I suck at bowling but I am really competitive so I was going to try to kick his ass. We arrived at the bowling alley, rented ugly bowling shoes and headed over to the first several lanes that were reserved for us. We all started drinking beer and eating the worst mozzarella sticks I have ever had.

We ventured out to find bowling balls and it was no surprise that Jake brought his own complete with a bag for it that had his initials on it. I should've known he actually owned one as well as his own bowling shoes. Jake was playing in the same lane as Jordie and the Managing Director, Steve. Before we could get started I had to find a kids bowling ball because I literally can't lift those other ones to which Matt and Jake found very amusing when I came back with a bright green kids ball weighing 15 pounds. It was the only one I could find because there were so many families here and not a lot of adults as most were out at bars or restaurants like normal people our age I guess. Our company was on the small side so we had about 6 lanes. Our group was split up but next to each other so we decided, whatever team gets the worst score has to do a shot before the next round. Matt then pulls me aside to remind me that we have a personal bet too and he wants to know what the winner will get. I told him I wasn't sure so he suggested the loser takes the other to dinner and has to pay and maybe we can then do a dinner/Skee-Ball night. I thought to myself is this just for fun or is this like a date but then I just let the thoughts go because honestly, the last thing Matt probably wants right now is a relationship seeing he just got out of one. I agreed on dinner and knew it would most likely be me paying for this dinner unless this 15 pound bowling ball had magic inside it.

After four games and I don't know how many beers, our team literally sucked and we ended up doing shots before every round. The awful part too is that the more I drank the worse I got and I literally wanted to put up the kids guards to avoid gutter balls but Matt wouldn't let me. He was reveling in the fact that he beat me and I owed him dinner. I told him a bets a bet and I would definitely take him to dinner. For the first time in a while, I was pretty drunk too. I normally only have a two drink limit because of my size but somehow I had managed to drink about five beers, did several shots and I barely ate anything except for that one gross mozzarella stick. I think we were all actually pretty drunk and it really sunk in when I hugged the guy that had rented my bowling shoes to me goodbye that I was wasted. Matt put my shoes on me and tied them like he was my parent. I kept telling everyone over and over that I don't really drink. Monica told me that maybe I just deserved a good night of being drunk to which I high fived her and almost fell over in the parking lot. We had all car-pooled over but I rode home with Matt because Matt had pretty much been the person holding me upright since we left the bowling alley. He was going to have to drive me home because I was in no shape to drive my car from the office back to my condo. Despite being drunk, I was actually quiet on our car ride. I really honestly just wanted to go to sleep.

When we arrived at my place, Matt walked me in, unlocked my door and placed my purse and keys on the kitchen counter, all while still holding me up. Then, he walked me up the stairs and brought me to my bedroom and helped me in bed, taking off my shoes and covering me with a blanket. I thanked him but passed out cold leaving him standing there and I heard him laugh a little at me. I also felt him give me a small kiss on my check and felt him run his fingers through my hair before he finally left but was too passed out to react. I think I got back up after he left and went to the bathroom and washed my face but never bothered to get out of my clothes and just passed out once again. I wasn't sure how I was going to get up for work the next day but I was glad the puppy had stayed at Roger's house tonight. When I woke up to my alarm the next morning, I just hoped I didn't make too much of a fool of myself at the holiday party. I had always heard stories of people that drink too much at these things and I couldn't believe I was now one of them. I hopped in the shower after taking two Advil and got ready for work while opening my Uber app and making arrangements for a ride. I texted Roger to check on the puppy and he said they were fine and I told him I would grab him before I left as we needed to give the puppy to the new owner today. I had found out last night that this family was going to have a two-part surprise because the puppy had come a little early and we figured, why make them wait?

I stopped by Roger's house to grab the puppy and his belongings and took the Uber to work since I didn't have my car from my escapades the night prior. When I got to my office Matt was waiting for me with a giant cup of Starbucks coffee. I thanks for him for his help last night as he grabbed the puppy from me and gave him kisses. I told him I owe him with my life for this much needed coffee. He laughed and told me he knew I was going to need this but was happy I am doing better. Monica peeked in and laughed at me too and we were all talking about the good time last night but also remembering the horrible food. Our conversation turned to this assignment and Matt told us that he had gotten about six celebrities and Jake had gotten about eight so far. A lot of the football players from the breakfast agreed to do it as well, so we were making progress. Matt told me he needed at least one or two really big names though to make this a big sensation. I knew he was right. I was forced to say goodbye to my puppy friend as the film crew was taking him now to do the delivery with Jake and Jordie accompanying them and I literally had to fight back tears for this little guy who wasn't even mine.

Just then, Bennie texted me that some of the high school friends I had seen over Thanksgiving weekend had sold pictures to TMZ of our get together and that it was posted on their site. When I had a free moment later that morning, I looked it up and saw us hanging out and having wine but the caption said "spoiled celebrity lifestyle" and I sighed. I hoped no one would see it. I was listed in there as well. Alexandria Thompson, daughter of Alexander Thompson, drinking a $600 per glass of Cabernet Sauvignon. I didn't even know what drink they offered me at my friend's home yet now I looked like I was just like my father only drinking the best of the best. I would've drank a glass of Cabernet Sauvignon that cost $11.00 for the whole bottle and been perfectly happy. The article labeling me the celebrity princess was weighing on my mind. Hopefully, no one will see it. It will be another file on my TMZ page but at least so far I made friends on my own here that I felt I could trust so maybe it wasn't such a bad thing if people knew the truth. It wasn't a deep, dark secret but I still preferred to be incognito, at least for now but I needed to share this part of me soon or I would start to look shady for hiding it this long and not confiding in them. Or risk them seeing an article like this, and then they would start to doubt me being genuine. Plus, I was always worried about them finding out and that alone was becoming too much to handle. I should know they will accept me. They didn't even flinch today about my drunken behavior last night and already had let it go.

Matt came back into my office as I was standing over my table organizing my Secret Santa prospects and asked if we wanted to do the dinner/Skee-Ball extravaganza this weekend on Saturday night. I smiled at him and told him yes. He asked me where we were going for dinner and I told him it would be a surprise because the truth is, I had no idea where to go! I looked up at Matt as he stood next to me. Matt was six foot two inches and I was only five foot two inches so I felt like I needed heels just to be around him but that was typical for me with any guy for the most part. Just then, my father texted me and let me know he would be in New York tomorrow and wanted to see me and take me to dinner Friday night and I could stay over at a hotel, have breakfast together and the car would take me back Saturday afternoon just in time for my night out with Matt. I couldn't believe it and I told Matt since he was standing next to me and saw my reaction to my father's text.

I shared my father's plans with Matt and let him know I would be back in time for our dinner. And, he said, "*So you are having dinner with the astronaut, mobster, FBI agent, alien*?" I just responded a playful "*yes*" as it was the truth! I could tell his statement came from curiosity about my father, thanks to Mercer. I was super excited that my dad had actually reached out to me and made plans. It felt like a Christmas miracle! He was taking me to dinner at Daniel, an expensive French restaurant in New York City that required a jacket and then we would stay overnight at a suite he booked for the weekend. He was in talks for another film and meeting with agents over the weekend but had actually told them he could only talk on Sunday to spend some time with me. For the first time, I felt like he was making an effort to spend time with his daughter.

Bennie would be there too which also made me jovial. It was close to the end of the day now and Jake had returned from the puppy surprise. We were looking forward to wrapping up the week and excited to get a break for the weekend. As excited as I was to see my father and Bennie, I was more excited for my night out with Matt.

When Friday finally arrived, Roger hung out with me while I packed and got ready that afternoon. He told me Matt was coming over to hang out and play video games and order pizza. Typical guys I thought in my head but I was glad Roger had found a friend in Matt and they could hang out without me being there. Roger told me he was missing the puppy and I agreed. I wanted to get one so bad but with work, I wasn't home enough. But, Roger was. He was home all the time but I guess needed time to concentrate when he did his art and it would be hard to focus with a little puppy. Roger said he was seriously considering adopting a dog anyway though and I hoped he did. I had my plans all figured out on what I was going to do with Matt the next day too so I looped in Roger and told him I was excited for this weekend. I had gotten a gift certificate to Surf Taco from the Secret Santa gift I chose for myself at work from under the tree so I figured I would put it to use. Luckily, we had a half-day this Friday as a part of our holiday party week perks so I was home earlier than usual this Friday afternoon. My dad texted me that the car would pick me up at 4:00 p.m. sharp, and I would meet up with Bennie in a private club where he would connect with us and then head over to the restaurant together. Everything was always so secretive with my dad and with paparazzi always on his tail, I understood why.

I was dressed in a Herve Leger off-the-shoulder little black dress with Jimmy Choo pumps and for a brief moment I felt like I was back in Hollywood. Roger walked out and waited with me for a few minutes at the elevator and as it opened there was Matt coming to hang out with Roger. "*Wow Ria! You look beautiful. Have fun tonight*" said Matt and I hugged him hello and thanked him for his kind words. I waved to them as the elevator door shut and I made my way down to the street to catch the car service. I saw Matt and Roger looking down and they waved goodbye again from Roger's window. I hopped in the car service and headed out. This time my dad sent a limo and it kind of pissed me off because I didn't want Matt seeing me getting into a limo. I tried to not let it spoil my mood and we hit the road. I stared out at the ocean as we drove away from Bradley Beach and was reminded of how happy I was to live in this little town by the sea.

Living on the Jersey coast was a little bit of a hike into New York City and with traffic and rush hour, we didn't get to the drop off spot until 6:00 p.m. in the evening. I texted Bennie that we were pulling up but I could already see him standing there in the cold waiting. I ran out of the car and hugged him and the driver told me to leave my bag in the car for now since this wasn't the hotel. Bennie and I went inside and headed up the elevator to a top floor and entered a private bar area with wall to wall glass windows showing the city sky scrapers shining brightly in the cold night. We sat down at a table and had some light snacks and refreshments until my father strolled in at 7:30 p.m. and gave me a hug. He tipped the server and charged it to his account, and we were on our way to the restaurant. I couldn't help but think I wouldn't mind being at Surf Taco right now but Daniel was an exquisite restaurant. We entered through a kitchen entrance and were whisked to a special room called the Sky Box that my father had reserved. In typical Alexander style, he had already ordered us an eight-course tasting menu at $1,600 per person. There was only three of us and they required a four person minimum so he paid an extra $1,600 for no one at all too.

After plates of pan-seared sea scallops, white sturgeon caviar, beef striploin with wild mushrooms and things I couldn't even pronounce, we were all stuffed. My dad filled us in on work. He is in talks for a huge movie project that will be a five part series with huge fan fare. He referenced it to the likes of *Twilight* and *The Hunger Games* but they hadn't decided on a name yet. He was the lead. That was no surprise to me but I also could tell he really wanted this role for some reason. He said this was very important to him and would be his best role yet. Just then Chef Daniel came out to say hello to us and gifted my father with a wide variety of condiments and candies from his upcoming catalog. It always amazed me that people who have so much money are the ones that get all of these types of things for free but then again, we did just spend almost $7,000 for dinner with tip. It wasn't until we got into the car and we were opening the candies from Chef Daniel to sample them that I noticed we were driving to the Lincoln Tunnel back towards New Jersey.

"*Where are we going? I thought we were going to a hotel?*" I asked. "*Don't get upset, darling. I can't end up having you stay overnight. I have to meet colleagues on this project for drinks later. It's all a part of the game and then we are doing brunch early with the director and others involved in the project*" replied my dad.

A single tear streamed down my face and Bennie put his arms around me and told me not to worry.

My father continued "*I am taking the time to drive all the way back to your condo with you to catch up only to turn around and have to drive all the way back to the city, aren't I?*" He sounded like he was doing me a favor. And, he was coming back to my condo to "drop me off" and hadn't even asked to see where I was living. I told him "*I just thought we would be spending the night together and having some quality time for once*". My dad appeared to ignore that comment and continued to just talk incessantly about the movie, about the woman he is seeing that I didn't even listen to because I know she will only last a month or two anyway. I couldn't even make eye contact with him. I felt so let down. I just stared out the window until we finally got into the Bradley Beach area. When we pulled up to the condo, it was 11:30 p.m.

"*What time exactly are you meeting for cocktails with an hour to hour and a half drive back*?" I yelled and just slammed the door grabbing my suitcase from the driver and not even saying goodbye to Bennie. He was full of shit. He just had the brunch and wanted a good night sleep and didn't care about me and spending the day with me tomorrow. My father followed me in calling my name. I was surprised he took the chance of someone recognizing him but there wasn't really anyone around with everyone out on a Friday night already.

"*Alexandria! Stop*!" he yelled and it echoed throughout condo complex. I immediately stopped, dropping my bag with my back towards him frozen. He hugged me from behind and said "*you know I love you. This business pulls me in so many directions. I don't mean to let you down. I have to go but I didn't mean to hurt you*".

I turned towards him and said "*that's the thing Dad...you put people in the business before me and I am your daughter. When your career dwindles, those people are going to call someone else and you will be alone. I am the one that would be there always. I think you should remember that*". I was upset but I hugged him anyway and walked towards the elevator and he yelled that he loved me and walked out. As I thought, he didn't ask me to come in and see my place. I got into the elevator and was thankfully alone. I fell down to the floor in a ball next to my bag and just cried. I felt like a child and worse though I felt unwanted. When the elevator door opened, Matt was standing there and immediately pulled me towards him.

"Ria, what happened? I heard the commotion and looked down and saw you arguing with I am guessing your father. Are you o.k.?" Matt hugged me sounding concerned. I cried into his shoulder and just told him *"He*

let me down. We went to dinner and then he returned me here and canceled our plans together for tonight and tomorrow. I'm sorry Matt that you have to see me like this. I'm just a mess." I wiped away my tears and pulled away from him. I felt bad dragging him into this and honestly, he has already done so much for me.

"Let me stay with you for a little while Ria, if you don't mind. This way we can talk about other things to take your mind off tonight and I can hopefully make you smile a little and then hopefully you will feel better tomorrow. Do you want to me to come in for a bit?" asked Matt. I just nodded and he picked up my bag and we entered my condo. I felt selfish but I wanted him to be with me. I asked him if Roger knew he was leaving but he said he would text him and let him know. Matt helped me unzip my dress and I went into the bathroom with my bag to change. My phone was blowing up with messages from Bennie and my dad but I just ignored them. Bennie never interfered with me and my father but I wish for once he could tell him to focus more on me. Bennie was more of a dad to me half the time. For all I knew, he did tell my father after I left but I would never know.

I came out and washed my face and Matt told me he liked me better without make-up on and I just said "*liar*" but he assured me he wasn't lying. He was laying on my bed naming expensive restaurants in the local area that I would treat him at tomorrow night trying to get me to laugh and I told him we would be doing something low-key but if really wanted expensive to tell me now. Matt told me he was fine with McDonalds and was just teasing. Thank God I thought since Surf Taco certainly wasn't fancy at all. It was well after midnight now and my thoughts in my head slipped out as I asked "*Matt, can you stay? You don't have to. Forget it*" but he immediately said yes, took off his shoes and his jeans and climbed into my bed in his boxers and t-shirt, and then hesitated and told me that he would sleep on the floor but I told him I didn't mind and slid in next to him. I thanked Matt for taking care of me and hugged him. I felt so good next to him, his body next to mine and being in his arms. As promised Matt changed the subject of my father and told me stories about his brother and that he is on a full baseball scholarship in college and has a great chance of being a major league player. Matt told me weird facts about himself like his middle name is Edward so I told him I was going to call Matt-E from now on and he laughed at me. It felt good in Matt's arms and with him next to me. He knew automatically how to cheer me up and make me forget about my worries. I was mentally exhausted but it was hard to fall asleep with his body so close to mine. I wanted him but I knew he would never do anything tonight. He knew I was fragile, and he was the kind of guy that put his heart before his physical needs. I wondered though if he thought of me in any other way than as merely as a friend. He was just getting out of a long-term relationship and for all I know, he has zero interest in getting into another. I wish we could finally show our feelings for each other.

We fell asleep and when I awoke, Matt was still sleeping so I slipped out of bed to go to the bathroom and head over to my kitchen to make breakfast. I felt bad that I made him stay and he slept in his clothes. But, I wanted him there too selfishly. Matt must have smelled the bacon and hunger kicked in as he strolled in and joined me for breakfast. "*Good morning beautiful*" he said to me and I couldn't help but blush as I gave him a hug. I told him I wanted to surprise him with breakfast to thank him for staying with me. We laughed over breakfast and talked about our upcoming Skee-Ball match tonight. He was convinced he would beat me but I assured him he would not. About an hour later, Matt told me he was going to head to his apartment to shower and run some errands before meeting back up with me so I gave Matt a big hug before he left and he held me a little too long for a normal hug but I thought maybe I was reading too much into it. Matt was always taking care of me, and I always felt so amazing when I was in his arms or next to him. He looked out for me at work, he helped me after I drank too much at the holiday party, and he was there for me last night. We let go of our embrace and he headed towards the elevator and I shut my door and smiled. I thought though about how Matt helped out Jordie too. Maybe it was just his nature to be helpful but deep down I knew he had gone above and beyond with me and I hoped I was different to him. I hoped he saw me as special and thought more of me than the way he saw Jordie. I took a shower and then invited Roger to come over so I could fill him in on the details of my night. I told him Matt stayed over but nothing happened. I wondered if Matt had confided anything in Roger about how he felt about me but Roger never gave me the indication that he did or maybe he didn't want to get in the middle.

Matt picked me up at 5:30 p.m. later that evening and I hopped in his truck. He looked handsome in a button down shirt with a brown suede jacket and casual pants. I brought him over to a Surf Taco restaurant near the ocean. Matt told me he loved this place as we walked through the doors. I then told him afterwards we could walk up to the Silverball Museum in Asbury Park, NJ on the boardwalk to compete like we did in bowling but this time in video games and, more importantly, Skee-Ball. Silverball Museum housed a large collection of iconic pinball games that you couldn't find anywhere and all of the old school video games as well as other games like air hockey and Skee-Ball. Matt brought out the fun side of me, and growing up Bennie and I always hit the arcade so I loved it. I didn't want to go to some fancy restaurant again like Daniel from last night and mostly I didn't want to make him feel like I was pressuring him into a date so I chose more of a low-key, fun approach to our night out.

The vibe in Surf Taco is relaxed and reminds me so much of life in California. Surfboard décor, surf competitions on the televisions and a cool Mexicali menu made it an easy, fun place to eat. Matt said this is one of his favorite spots as we ordered smoothies and fish tacos and sat at a small table and talked while we waited for our food. I was so happy this night had finally arrived and more importantly, we were finally alone. Matt told me his younger brother is his mini-me but much more athletic. He also told me a little more about his ex-girlfriend, Linda. He said they dated for a few years but were just always together because their families are friendly. He said they know each other like a brother and sister would but there was just never any physical chemistry for him and it just felt forced by their families' desire to see them together. He told me that Linda shows up places that he frequents, and texts him nightly to talk or check on his day, and he found it super annoying but understandable. And, although he will obviously always be friends with her, it just doesn't allow him to move on and she doesn't get the hint. He said she often finds out where he is going and he just feels like she has been taking it too far with her hope to get back together as it will never happen. I felt better knowing he was closing that chapter of his life.

Matt kept asking me about my family so I felt like I should share too and talked to him a little more about the loss of my mom. Matt held my hand as I told him the story of her passing. I hadn't really talked about it in a long time with details except more recently with Roger. I was so little when it happened and it was like she just disappeared and it was never the same after that. My mom had stopped modeling shortly after I was born only taking a few assignments like Sports Illustrated and we were together all the time. But, once I started school, she did some modeling assignments again more frequently and during one shoot had hurt her back and been prescribed pain medication. Who would've known this pain medication would cause her addiction and eventual death. It's still hard for me to even take an Advil when I have a headache because of it. It was so hard to grow up with my mother not being there. I told him it was hard to not have her in my life and missing those mother/daughter moments that I had so yearned for. Speaking of mother/daughter moments, I made a mental note that I still owed McKenna a butter cookie night and I didn't want to forget.

Matt shared that he had a cousin, although distant, that was fighting a battle as well and was recently diagnosed with cancer. He told me that life is short and he could understand my pain with the loss of my mother. He told me his cousin is only fourteen years old and has a huge battle ahead of him and it's going to be a difficult journey. He switched gears to get away from all the dark talk and asked me what my father did for a living and I hesitated and he could tell. That only made it worse and he said '"*c'mon – is he a drug lord or in the FBI*?" to which I replied "*yes*" since technically as an actor he has played both those roles but luckily our food arrived and the subject changed. I did tell him that my father worked in the movie business but didn't elaborate. I just told him that he wasn't around much so I had been looking forward to finally spending some time with him. "*And, he let you down last night. I have to say Ria, if I could be with someone like you, I would never let you go, spend every second with you and most definitely would never let you down. I am so sorry that he did that to you.*" This time I blushed and I gave him a kiss on the cheek.

After our casual meal at Surf Taco, we decided to walk to the boardwalk only a few blocks up where Skee-Ball awaited. But, we started running instead because it was freezing and Matt paid for us to get into the Silverball Museum and we were still shivering. We put on our wristbands, warming up from the cold, and felt like little kids as we made our way to the Ms. Pacman machine. I don't mean to brag but I have a pattern for every one of the boards on this game and he isn't going to be able to touch my score and I was right. He couldn't pass the first two boards to my evil delight. I had already secured myself as the champion in the world of Pacman, and he admitted his defeat as we left those video games and wandered around. We had to wait a while but finally we got our opportunity at Skee-Ball. Growing up, I used to be really good at this game and no one could ever beat me. Matt told me he was really good too but I wasn't afraid. Matt and I went head to head and were only 10 points apart but I beat him in the first round. He said "*two out of three*" but I won the next round too so I told him he should just end the misery and quit. He laughed and bowed down to me as the winner that I was, and we made our rounds trying vintage pinball machines with themes from everything like *Charlie's Angels* to the band *KISS.* Both of us had a sore on our thumb from the video game joystick so we decided to leave and began running back to the car to get out of the cold as soon as possible. We immediately got into the car, turning on the heat and hugged one another to warm up until the heated seats finally kicked in and we were on the road back to Bradley Beach. Will he ever kiss me? I loved hugging him but I was ready for a kiss. Matt asked if I wanted to stop by a bar on the way home and have a drink so I said yes. There was no way I wanted this night to end so soon.

We laughed the whole car ride back to the bar about his poor Skee-Ball skills and his even worse abilities at Ms. Pac Man but he reminded me that I bowl with a children's bowling ball and need the guards to not get a gutter ball, and I couldn't help but agree. This was my kind of date. Eating at a low-key, casual restaurant and doing something simple and fun were the times where I had the best times. When we arrived back near Bradley Beach, we stopped in a bar called D'Arcy's and got two seats at the bar and ordered drinks. Matt reached over and held my hand making me blush and he told me in my ear "*I had so much fun tonight Ria*" and I leaned into his ear and said "*me too Matt*" and our faces were close enough that I thought the kiss I was waiting for was about to happen. The bartender placed the drinks in front of us but neither cared or took our eyes off each other as Matt came closer and I just knew this was it. "*You are the most beautiful girl I have ever seen Ria*" and he started to lean in pulling me closer to him. "*I adore you Matt*" I answered.

But, Matt stopped suddenly and looked over his shoulder as someone must have tapped him on it, and we both look to see Linda was standing there. I didn't think it was much of a coincidence she was randomly standing there alone at a bar that Matt probably went to often just as he was about to kiss me. It was apparent she still loved him, and was basically stalking him. Part of me couldn't blame her for not wanting to let Matt go. I think she just needed to realize that she would always have him in her life but accept that it would only be as a friend or she was going to lose him completely. Matt excused himself looking frustrated and went over to another part of the bar to talk to her. He was super discouraged as he got up and I could see him upset with her as they talked. I took a sip of my drink and knew for sure that I was falling in love with Matt. I was hoping for that kiss that never seemed to be able to happen. We were so close…

Chapter 8
A KISS LIKE NO OTHER

Our drinks had arrived so I took another sip and waited for Matt to return. I pulled out my mirror from my purse to check my hair and make-up. I wore my hair down in beach waves and had worn a simple but flattering long sleeved t-shirt and cute jeans. I don't know why I felt nervous and worried about what I was going to wear to go play Skee-Ball but I always wanted to look good for Matt for some reason. Matt returned and I tried to be playful and act like I wasn't bothered by Linda's interruption and said "*welcome back Matt-E*" and he apologized. "*This girl will just not leave me alone. I know it sounds bad because I don't hate her but it's just so annoying that she is always in my shadow and always coming by. She is always thinking I am just going to get back together with her. She can't move on*" confided Matt. "*You are always cheering me up so now it's finally my turn to do something for you. Where is she now?*" I asked and Matt told me she was in the bathroom.

"*Do you want to give her a hint that you're not interested?*" I asked. "*Yes, please. I am open to any ideas to get her to keep her distance. What did you have in mind?*" responded Matt. I pulled Matt up from the chair and over near the wall. I grabbed his hands and put them on my waist and threw my arms around his neck while on my tippy toes since he was so tall. "*When she comes out of the bathroom, she will look over to find you. She will see you and me in this position and think - yikes they are together. I think she will leave pretty quickly unless you think this is too harsh*?" I slyly asked.

"*No. I like this. More than you probably know*" Matt stated with a clever raise of his eyebrows and then hesitated still in each other's embrace and looking at me right in the eyes. "*I want to kiss you, Ria*" he says softly. "*To scare off Linda? Or, in this moment*?" I asked with fear in my heart. "*In this moment. In fact from the moment we met*" Matt whispers "*unless you don't want me to*?" "*I want you to. I've wanted that from the moment we met too*" I quickly whisper back as Matt leans in.

The moment was finally here. Our lips touch and he kisses me with small, soft kisses until our tongues enter each other's mouths and the romantic kiss becomes more intense as he passionately kisses me and moves his hands from my waist, up my back and through my hair. He kisses me hard on the lips and pulls me in for a hug and our bodies are so close we felt like one person. He brings me back to face him and leans his forehead on mine and kisses me again softly on the lips.

"*Ria. I have wanted to kiss you from the moment I saw you. You are the most beautiful girl on this planet. Inside and out.*" Matt shares. "*Matt. You are amazing. I've wanted to kiss you too. You are all I ever think about*" I shared and I truly meant it. Matt hugged me again and we smiled at each other and looked at our drinks sitting over on the bar. Neither of us even looked to see if Linda had seen our romantic moment and we just put money on the bar and left the drinks there. It was getting late and there was no sense hanging out at a bar with Matt's ex-girlfriend in our shadow so we headed the short drive back to my condo holding hands the entire way. Matt walked me to my door when he dropped me off and kissed me goodbye. Our kisses were so intense and when he left I felt like a teenager as I closed the door behind me. I wanted to ask him in and pull his clothes off but I know Matt didn't operate that way. Matt meant everything to me. He really is the man of my dreams. I texted

Claire and told her we finally kissed and she called me immediately to discuss the details and then I headed to bed. I was head over heels crazy for this man and he meant everything to me.

Matt texted me the next morning with a clip from the Thomas Rhett song called "*Die a Happy Man*" and the lyrics said "*Last night, was hands down, one of the best nights, that I've had no doubt, between the bottle of wine, and the look in your eyes and the Marvin Gaye, then we danced in the dark under September stars in the pourin' rain, and I know that I can't ever tell you enough, that all I need in this life is your crazy love, if I never get to see the Northern lights, or if I never get to see the Eiffel Tower at night, oh, if all I got is your hand in my hand, Baby, I could die a happy man*" and he told me that kissing me last night was the best night of his life and I literally wished he was here so that I could melt into his arms. I texted him back "*Oh Matt. How did I get so lucky*?" as I felt my eyes tearing. "*I'm the lucky one, Ria. You mean everything to me*" Matt answered. This didn't even seem real? I had fallen so hard for Matt in such a short amount of time and he seems to have also fallen for me. I could barely concentrate all day thinking about Matt. His romantic gesture with the song and his loving words made me feel the happiest I have ever felt in my entire life. He was all I could think about and I couldn't wait to kiss him again and again and again. I wanted to invite him over and spend the day again with him but he had mentioned to me that he was helping his mom move some furniture today so I would have to wait until work on Monday to see him. It's funny when you are in love how the world just seems so much better. I bought fresh flowers for my kitchen table, baked cookies and walked around smiling all day. I don't think anything could top this feeling.

It was back to work on Monday and Monica immediately noticed what was happening between myself and Matt. It was hard not to recognize that we were falling in love with each other. Even Jake made a few sarcastic comments when he was around us trying to get us to stop looking at anyone else but each other. I wasn't sure how the whole office romance thing was going to go over with Jordie so we tried our best to hide it from her but it was hard to stay away from each other. At lunch that day, I ran over to the Children's Hospital to check in on Billy and to see if I could find the patient that I had made the anonymous donation to and to walk by his room and try to see how he is doing. I could only hope my donation would make a difference. I knew it couldn't cure him but the pressure of not having the money to pay for his treatment would hopefully help them be more positive. I got to the children's floor and had dropped off a few boxes of candy canes for the nurses and then took a walk down the hall. I wanted to pop in to see our friend Billy but his room was empty so he must have been somewhere else having treatment or an exam. As I exited the room, I bumped right into Matt and he quickly hugged and kissed me. "*What are you doing here?*" I asked. "*I was going to try and stop by to see my cousin real quick. He is the one I was telling you about at Surf Taco. He has a rare bone cancer but the family wanted us to come by for some news. Will you come with me?*" asked Matt. Bone cancer I asked myself in my head? Could Matt's cousin be the boy I anonymously donated to? It can't be. Or, what if the news was grim like he wasn't going to make it? I didn't know if I could stand to hear the news but I agreed to be there for Matt.

Matt and I entered his room. A woman came up and hugged Matt and she introduced herself to me as Owen's mom, Mary. Matt introduced me and then I looked over and saw Owen in his hospital bed smiling and I shook his hand immediately recognizing him from the GoFundMe page photos. I breathed a sigh of relief that he seemed to be o.k. Matt pulled Mary aside and told her we couldn't stay long because we had to get back to work. Mary told everyone to be quiet and as about eight of us waited to hear what she was going to say, I already knew what it would be. Mary started "*We received word that a guardian angel has answered our prayers. While Owen still has a long battle ahead of him, we are excited to announce that we had an anonymous donor who paid off our entire GoFundMe page for his medical expenses.*" Everyone screamed, cheered, cried and hugged each other. I couldn't believe it. I was the Secret Santa to Matt's cousin. I hugged Mary and then Matt and gave Owen a kiss on the cheek before leaving. Matt stayed a few minutes after to celebrate with his family so I told him I would meet him back at the office and when I made it back to my car tears streamed down my face. I had made a difference and I could never have imagined it would also impact the man I was falling in love with. Life works in mysterious ways.

I saw Jordie when I got back to the office so I asked her how the puppy made out with his new family and she told me they were absolutely thrilled and she seemed super happy telling me too. I didn't tell her that Matt told me it was her sister's family because I didn't want to break his confidence in me or her confidence in Matt either but I was glad to see Jordie appear happy for once. I made it back up to my office as we were all hard at work at Secret Celebrity Santa. We had lined up all of our celebrities and tied them to a needy family or someone who had done an act of kindness. There was really just one person left that we needed to resolve. There was another boy that I had met in the children's hospital named Billy though who we wanted to do something for. Billy had a heart condition that caused him to have multiple surgeries. I had tried to see him earlier today but he wasn't in his room. His hero was Superman. His hospital room was covered with Superman pictures and figurines. My dad had played Superman in one of the movies out last year and Billy was obsessed with the Superman version of my father. I knew I could make his year or even his life if I told my father about the Secret Celebrity Santa project that I was working on. There was a lot of pressure on Matt to find a celebrity to be the Secret Santa for Billy and I had to decide if I would be willing to do it. Should I finally tell Matt about my father? I knew I had to tell Matt about my father eventually. I was lying to him and it wasn't how I wanted to start our relationship. My father was unpredictable though and while he could let me down, I wasn't sure I could deal with the fallout of him letting Billy down.

Roger came over one night after work to hang out and he told me that I needed to tell Matt the truth. Not only would I be helping out Billy, but I couldn't keep this from Matt of all people now that we had finally started seeing each other. I knew he was right. I didn't want to jeopardize my relationship with Matt by starting it out with keeping secrets from him. I called my father that night after Roger left. He had signed up to do this 5-part movie he had been telling me about at our dinner the other night and was starting immediately and would be filming mainly from New York City so he would be in the area. I just wondered if I could count on him to show up. At first my father said he wasn't sure if he had the time. This was the only thing I had ever asked of my father. "*Dad, I never ask you for anything but this boy Billy loves you and Superman. He has a life-threatening heart condition and you meeting him and bringing him gifts would make such an impact on him and his focus on his recovery. I need you to do this for me. It would be an hour or two of your time and you will be in New York*" I pleaded. *"Alexandria, you know how busy I am*" was his answer at first. "*This could be good publicity for you"* I told him. There was a hesitation after that comment and I knew his ego would not be able to say no when I made it about him sadly. He finally said "*okay, I'll do it*" and I told him "*I love you. You are making such a difference. This means so much to me and to Billy too!*" Just don't let me down, I thought in my head. This wasn't about me anymore, this was about Billy. I was not about to crush this boy's dreams with all of the challenges he is already facing. Now that my dad had agreed, I told Bennie as well to make sure he held my father accountable to being there. I knew Bennie would help me make this happen if he could. There was only one thing left for me to do and that was to tell Matt.

Speaking of not crushing little kids dreams, I called Monica to see if I could come over tomorrow night to bake cookies with McKenna if they didn't have plans and she excitedly agreed. I went over to the grocery store to get my supplies so that they wouldn't have to use their stuff and I purchased sugar, flour, butter, baking powder, salt, vanilla, tin foil and even a few cookie sheets and anything else I could think of that we may need including tons of sprinkles and icing for decorating. I was excited to spend time with my little friend and I wanted to make it special for her. I drove home and told Matt of my plans and he told me he wanted to come help too but was driving to pick his brother up from college tomorrow night and that we would just do it ourselves another time. I am always up for cookies so that sounded good to me. I had to make the dough for the cookies today as it was supposed to be made in advance and chilled and then it could sit at room temperature for a while to make it easier to roll for cutting and shaping with cookie cutters. Tomorrow all day at work we had a mandatory training and compliance day so we couldn't do any work on our project, and I didn't address my father and the news yet and figured I would make plans to tell Matt the following day in the morning over coffee so that I could tell him first before sharing with the team. I had thought my plans were set and crossed my fingers that Matt would be o.k. with the news. I knew I could just call and tell him right now and I was making it worse on myself. But, for some reason I dreaded it and having a plan to do it in person when we weren't so busy felt better.

Matt left work early to go pick up his brother from college and had a big drive ahead of him. I headed home, taking out the dough so that it would be room temperature by the time I got to Monica's house, and then ate dinner. I put the dough in my bag and then gathered up my baking items and decorating supplies and traveled the short five minute drive to Avon-by-the-Sea to Monica and Robbie's house. McKenna was already at the door before I even had a chance to park my car in anticipation for my arrival. It was just us girls tonight as Robbie was at a landscaping conference this week and Monica's mom had already left for the day. McKenna and I set up all the supplies while Monica pre-heated the oven to 350 degrees. We floured her kitchen island so that the dough wouldn't stick and used a rolling pin to roll out a large piece of the dough and I showed McKenna how to use the cookie cutters and cut out shapes. We placed the cutouts on baking sheets that were lined with aluminum foil so that the cookies wouldn't stick and also so that the messy decorations that miss the cookie could easily be cleaned up later. McKenna excitedly cut the cookies and I showed her how to decorate a few to give her some ideas and then she was busy at work making her master cookie design creations.

"*So, how are things with Matt? You are guys are officially together, right?*" asked Monica. "*Things are incredible Monica. I love that man and I hope it is official and exclusive. We haven't really talked about it since it's so new still and we have been so busy but I have never been happier, and he is just so damn perfect*!" I responded. "*You guys are perfect and Robbie and I are thrilled of course. I love you guys together. I have known Matt a while and I have never seen him so in love before. I think it's pretty safe to say it is definitely exclusive*" replied Monica. "*I hope you are right Monica. I have never felt this way about anyone in my entire life. I have one thing I need to tell him, and you too, about myself and in particular about my family and upbringing. I am worried of his reaction but I want to tell him first before I tell you, but I plan on telling the team tomorrow. It's just something I don't know will sit well with Matt and I cannot lose him*" I confided. "*I understand but what could it possibly be? I think it's pretty clear how Matt feels but sounds like you are doing the right thing by telling him first and I think it will all work out*" Monica finished.

It took about two and a half hours and we finally finished all of our butter cookies and had several trays of them. I took one plateful to give to Roger and another one for Matt (and snuck a few for myself too) but let McKenna keep the rest to give to friends and family. She was only in a nursery school but I told her to put some in little baggies and share with her classmates if she was allowed by her teachers. She loved that idea. After working all day and baking all night, I headed home to take a bubble bath and relax. I texted Claire to say hello. She was just getting out of work with the time zone difference. Matt texted me as well letting me know he made it safely to pick up his brother and making sure I saved him some cookies. I got out of the bath and headed to take a look out my window to see the ocean and noticed some flurries coming down. This was not something you would see in California unless you went to the mountains to ski. I watched in awe as the light flurries covered the street and the sand. Like Roger's picture, I wanted to take the time to look around and see the beauty all around me. I had never really been around a lot of snow. I was in love with snow and all of its charm although I am sure driving in it isn't much fun. I was becoming a true Jersey Girl.

Monica had sent me a picture of thirty baggies tied with a ribbon that McKenna insisted on her making to bring to her nursery school class tomorrow. I was happy that she had so much fun and I loved that little girl. Monica told me she was exhausted but to see McKenna so happy made it all worth it. I was worried about Matt driving in the snow but she told me it was just a coating to an inch of snow and I shouldn't worry. I was so not used to this snow thing so I had to google the weather channel to understand what a coating even meant but felt better about Matt's travels after reading about it. I got another text from Lynne telling me to turn on the news. The family I had helped by paying off their GoFundMe page were featured on the news for their anonymous donation receipt. They went to the media to say thank you and how life-changing this was for their family not to have to worry about the expense ahead of them and just focus on their son's recovery. They pleaded to know who the donor was but I my lips were sealed. I smiled and texted Lynne back that I wasn't sure who did that but it was wonderful and put a wink emoji. Lynne just said goodnight and I watched the news story and googled more information about snow before heading to bed. I made another mental list to buy gloves, a hat and scarf. I didn't even own any of those things being a California girl, but now I was a New Jersey Girl and I was ready to embrace all of what that meant.

Chapter 9
ROLE OF A LIFETIME

I had let my daughter down and ruined her night. Alexander Thompson – you've done it again! But, the director told me to stop by and meet up with my potential love interest in this time travel movie for a cocktail around midnight and I didn't want to tell him no. It was the only time she could do it because she was coming from another movie set and had zero time. Boy did that sound familiar to me. It was the story of my life as well. They had also moved my meeting with them to a brunch on Saturday morning instead of the Sunday we had committed to. This now meant I had to break my plans with my daughter. I didn't even have the heart to tell her until I was forced to because she noticed we were heading into the Lincoln Tunnel and away from New York City on her own. Despite agreeing to meet up with my potential future co-star at midnight, I had taken a risk and put my daughter first too at least by going along for the ride and driving her home. I was going to be late to meet my potential co-star but Alexandria was more important and I had already crushed her by changing our plans.

I made it back into the City by 12:30 a.m. to meet up with the beautiful Veronica Chambers at a bar named Beautique on 58th Street in their lounge. I had been here once before and it was a premium cocktail lounge, and most importantly, it was very private. "*I know I am late Veronica but I have a good reason*" I started. Veronica and I had met multiple times before. The Hollywood elite was a small world and a tight knit circle once you made it to our level. She was in many movies and we had acted together before although never as each other's love interest. I knew I could get her to understand or at least forgive me. "*I had made plans with my daughter. We had dinner tonight and she was supposed to stay over in the city and spend time with me tomorrow but as you know our meeting with the team for the table read got moved to tomorrow morning instead of Sunday.*" Veronica challenged me and responded with "*I know I am annoyed they changed it to tomorrow too because I had made multiple plans that I had to then have canceled but that still doesn't explain why you are late Alexander.*" I was honest for once and responded with the truth "*My daughter was upset with me. I haven't been in her life as much as I should through the years. All I do is work and I made these plans with her on my own for the first time and she was excited only for me to crush her once again and change them. But, I couldn't just leave after dinner and not spend any time with her so I drove with her in the car service to drop her off but it was an hour ride there and back to the City. The good thing is that there was not much traffic but the distance caused me to be about a half hour late to meet with you. I had already canceled the time tonight and tomorrow with her so I hope you can understand.*"

I had won Veronica over. She was a mother and she worked just as much as me, so I know of all people she would understand. Veronica and I reviewed our storyline and discussed how to make our on-set chemistry convincing for tomorrow. I needed to nail this. I haven't had to actually read or try out for a part in a few years so it was one of those good "get your ego in check" moments. We parted ways to get at least a few hours of sleep and then met up with the crew for brunch at 11:00 a.m. the next morning. Morning arrived and I arrived at the brunch. After we ate, we had our scripts in hand to do our table read. The scene was when I had to break it to Veronica's character about my assignment and that by me doing this time travel, I was about to risk the possibility of losing her by changing the future. This was the most intense scene in the movie so we had to nail it and have chemistry, or we weren't going to be the right actors for these roles. Although we already technically had the parts, they could decide still that we would be out if we didn't connect well together. Veronica was very easy to have chemistry with. Through the years, I had always thought she was beautiful. I admired her confidence too. She was a business woman, a terrific actress, a mother and a friend. But, she had been married for a long time so there was no chance of a pursuit. She divorced for the first time earlier this year and was finally single. Maybe spending time with her was perfect timing to explore something between us for the first time. We seemed to be very similar people.

We started the table read scene in front of the creative team, the director and investors in the movie. There have been many hired talent in this industry who had been let go after a table read. Maybe they challenged the material, or maybe they acted unprofessionally just reading and not acting the part, but I was going to give it my all and show them I was made for this part. My character was Adam and Veronica's character was Lily. We were a married couple starting our life together but living in a very difficult time where residents lived in fear.

Scene.

Lily is alone in her kitchen drinking a coffee. She has her head leaning into her hands with a look of despair. She knows the world as she knows it may change but it's not the only thing she is worried about. She would most likely lose Adam. Adam is the only man she has ever loved. The bedroom door opens and Adam walks into the kitchen dressed and ready to leave on his trip. He runs over to Lily and hugs her.

<u>Adam</u>

You need to trust me Lily. If there is any way that I can help it, I will find a way to make sure that we are together.

<u>Lily</u>

Can't they send someone else? Why does it have to be you? I can't lose you Adam. Not now and not ever.

<u>Adam</u>

You know why it has to be me. I have to do this. I am the only one who has built the relationship with this regime. I am the only one who can stop this. I am risking everything important in my life to help save the rest of the millions of people who live under this horrible regime. As much as I want to say no, you know why I can't. I have to do this Lily. I don't want to lose you though. You know that. You know you are everything to me. I am sorry you are scared. So am I Lily. So am I.

Pause.

Lily grabs a letter she has written for Adam off of the kitchen island and places it in his pocket.

<u>Lily</u>

This is important Adam but I don't want you to read it until you are in the new dimension.

<u>Adam</u>

What is it? You are scaring me.

Lily places her finger over his lips to quiet Adam. She has news indeed but if he reads this letter now, he will never leave and she knew he was indeed the only person to stop this regime. She knew she would probably lose him but she also knew he deserved to know what could've been.

Lily

It's not bad. It's good. Just promise me you will wait to read it.

Adam

I promise Lily.

Adam hugs Lily while Lily sobs in his arms. This may be the last time they will ever see each other but not if Adam can help it. A beep is heard outside.

Adam

I have to go. They are here to pick me up. I love you Lily. Until next time?

Lily

I love you Adam. Until next time.

Lily and Adam squeeze each other's hands and their fingers slowly part as Adam heads to the door to the men awaiting him. Lily looks from the window watching his car pull away. She wonders if she will even remember this moment once Adam travels back in time to change the future.

End Scene.

Veronica and I were so lost in the scene, we forgot we were even at a table read. We both had tears in our eyes and were lost in the moment. The creative team in the room started to clap and cheer. We had nailed it. Veronica and I were meant to be Adam and Lily. We more than nailed the part, it was a homerun and we were both hired officially on the spot.

I knew that Alexandria couldn't possibly realize how much this made me happy but I was excited to be over in the east coast by my little girl for a while. The only issue is some filming needed to start next week to get a few things filmed while New York was all decorated for the holidays. The good news is that my house in Spring Lake was going to have some guests soon, and I could be by Alexandria pretty quickly. The bad news is that I didn't get even a little break before jumping from one project right into the next.

When Alexandria called me to ask me about doing the Secret Celebrity Santa. I wanted to say yes on the spot. It was going to make a huge difference in so many lives and I would be supportive to my daughter in her role as well as for this young boy, Billy. But, I had just gotten this job and it was my very first week of work and I would already have a demand if I told them I had to leave for a few hours. It was early enough in the production that they could fire me if I wasn't careful as they had an out clause in my contract because of my prior on-set meltdown. But, I could hear how much this meant to her in her voice so I said yes. I would figure out a way to make myself available. It was about time that I gave back to the community too. I had been wanting to do something anyway and this was a great place to start, helping my daughter.

Despite all of these things happening in my life, I felt change coming. It was a good change though. I was finally coming into my own as I approached the age of fifty. Even though I still played the role of a thirty year old to help me recapture my youth and gave me the reminder of feeling young, the reality is that I am not thirty anymore. Being around Veronica felt good too. I could tell we have a connection and maybe for the first time, I can settle down again and focus on a relationship. Alexandria was going to see a new version of her father. The real version. The one that has been here all along and is finally revealing himself, and I couldn't wait to finally be the man I was always meant to be.

Chapter 10
MISSION SECRET SANTA

The next day in the office was the day I was going to finally tell Matt about my father. I couldn't wait any longer because the Secret Celebrity Santa was coming up fast. I needed to tell them before alternate plans were made for Billy and I know my plan will be MUCH better for Billy. But not only that, it was time for me to face Matt and share the truth. He deserved that and in fact "we" deserved that as a couple if we were ever going to start off our relationship the right way. I just don't know why I am so nervous. It's probably because Matt means everything to me. When I arrived at Shore Events, I saw Matt in his office on the phone and tried to motion to him that I needed to speak to him but he mouthed the words "*it's going to be a while*" and blew me a kiss as I handed him a plate of cookies from last night. My heart was racing because I knew I needed to tell him now. Of all days, he has to be on an urgent call this early in the morning! I tried one more time to grab Matt before our team meeting to tell him first but he was on that conference call still. Our meeting had started and Matt was late from being stuck on a call so we had to start without him. I had no choice and was left with a pit in my stomach. The subject came up of Billy just as Matt walked through the doors. I struggled to find the words because this was not what I had planned and I didn't want Matt to find out like this but I was forced to tell him along with the others in the meeting. This wasn't how I wanted this to happen because I knew he would have liked it better if I told him alone, in person and made it more meaningful.

I shared the news that I was able to book Alexander Thompson otherwise known as Superman to come in for Billy. "*Holy Shit*" said Monica, "*that's incredible. How did you do it*?" Jake immediately put two and two together. "*Wait a minute. Ria, are you AlexandRIA Thompson, daughter of Alexander Thompson, the actor*?" I could see the look on Matt's face as he didn't even sit but appeared to sink into his chair at the prospect of what he was hearing when Jake asked me. I couldn't deny it. I was doing this for Billy but I had wanted to tell Matt myself first but never got the chance so I just held my head high and gave a firm answer. "*Yes, he is my father. I don't talk about it much because I want to be treated like everyone else*." "*That's amazing Ria*" chimed in Monica and as Roger predicted, she was super supportive. As the meeting ended, Matt quickly exited the room. I called out to him and said "*Matt, I was trying to tell you first this morning*" but he hurriedly left and went to his office and shut the door. I texted Matt and told him the same thing that I had tried to tell him first this morning but he was on the phone but he didn't respond to me. The cat was out of the bag and now I had to live with the consequences. I didn't want Matt to think I didn't care enough about him to tell him everything about me. That was the farthest thing from the truth and I was about to tell him. I was under a time crunch with booking my father since the Secret Santa event was in two days.

Monica came by and gave me a hug. "*So, this was what you were referring to last night, right?*" she asked and I nodded. "*And, I am guessing you didn't get to tell Matt just yet either based on his reaction?*" she continued and tears ran down my face so she knew the answer. "*Listen Ria. We love you no matter what. You could be from the poorest family or the richest family. None of that matters to us. Matt is a very sensitive guy. Just give him some time to let it sink in. He is probably hurt because of all people, you didn't tell him right away but trust me when I say that he is not going to want to lose you. He probably needs time to process it all. Don't give up on him.*" I couldn't even speak and

I hugged her one more time and she slipped out leaving me alone trying but failing terribly to work.

Matt finally emerged from his office with a printout in his hand. He came into my office and shut my office door. I was scared to death staring at Matt and knowing I never wanted to lose him. The paper he had in hand looked familiar right away. It was from my TMZ page. He had the article calling me a spoiled brat that only drinks expensive wine. He lay the paper in front of me on my desk. "*I didn't think this was the girl I was falling in love with. You played me for a fool. We are from different worlds and the things that are important to you are* ***so*** *unimportant to me. We don't belong together*" he told me as he held back a mixture of anger and tears. I tried to interject but he wouldn't even let me speak or get a word in. He opened my door and exited and promptly left for the day. I started to cry and Monica came in, closing the door behind her, and comforted me. "*I didn't mean for this to happen. I wanted to start a life for myself as simply me and not the daughter of Alexander Thompson. These images that Matt brought to me is not who I am"* I said showing her the TMZ handout and explaining how I stopped to see those friends and was there for not even an hour having no clue what wine I was even drinking. *"It's far from who I have ever been as a person despite having everything I did growing up*" I pleaded to Monica and she hugged me. Monica looked me directly in the eyes and told me "*Just give him some time Ria. It's a lot to take in and he loves you so much so he is just hurt. Give him some space and then try to talk to him. I have known Matt for a while and I think he is just a little hurt that you didn't tell him everything right away but I think after he thinks about it, he will understand why you didn't. I mean, you are right, if you would have come into Shore Events as Alexander Thompson's daughter, would we have viewed you differently? I certainly hope not, but its human nature to look up to people in the spotlight. And, if Matt liked you, a part of you would've questioned if it was because of your father. It wouldn't have* *been true but it would've crossed your mind. Now, you know he loves you for you. He will get over this if he wants to be with you. Regardless, you did the right thing for Billy by telling us and that alone should show Matt the real person you are inside*" she finished. Monica was so caring and such a good friend. I just hoped she was right.

I tried to text Matt at night before bed but he didn't respond so I took Monica's advice and stopped bothering him. I arrived before anyone would be at work the following day and just went into my office and was trying to get things done in case my emotions got the best of me once Matt arrived. Today was the final day of preparations for Secret Celebrity Santa and I just hoped all went smoothly so that all of our hard work would pay off and all of these stories had happy endings tomorrow. Matt arrived but he just ignored me the entire day. We didn't have any meetings so I just stayed in my office and Monica and Jake came in a few times to discuss things but I never left my office, not even to eat lunch. I was avoiding Matt and he was obviously wanting nothing to do with me. I knew Monica said to give him time to have it sink in but I couldn't take it for much longer. At the end of the day, I was starving and tired but all seemed in place for tomorrow's festivities. It was going to be so amazing and yet I didn't even feel like attending. I locked up my office at the same time as Matt. I looked over at him but he didn't even look my way. I lingered so he could go down the elevator without me and then left shortly after and by the time I got to my car, he was long gone. I sunk into my car seat and cried once again.

I couldn't leave things like this with Matt. He was too important to me but I couldn't change who I was either. He either had to accept it and forgive me for not telling him, or let me go. I preferred the first option because he really was the one I wanted for the rest of my life. I knew it from the moment I set eyes on him at the movie night before I even knew he was going to work with me. I couldn't bear to lose him and even thought that if he couldn't forgive me, I might resign and go back to California because I couldn't even bare to see him every day if he didn't want me. I suddenly knew how Linda must feel. I couldn't imagine not being with Matt for the rest of my life, even if we had only known each other a few months. What was I going to do? I called Roger from my car and he tried to console me and tell me it was going to work out, but I felt nothing but pain.

It was finally the day of Secret Celebrity Santa. This incredible event had finally arrived so I tried my best to stay positive. I texted Bennie to ensure my father was going to show up as Billy was the last stop of the day and I would kill him if he didn't come and reveal himself to Billy. Bennie assured me he would be there and he would accompany him as well so that we could see each other, and to of course ensure that my father stuck to the plan. I needed my father to follow through on this for me. It wasn't just for me, he would be letting down Billy and I couldn't let that happen. I tried my best to avoid Matt and give him the time he needed to let my father sink in with him. I was dying inside as we started our day and this was the kind of day that would normally be one of the best moments of my life. I just couldn't get over the pain of being in a fight with Matt. A camera crew followed us around as we made rounds either delivering gifts with video messages from the recipients' celebrity version of Secret Santa or in some cases, the celebrity joined us as well. We traveled all over parts of the Jersey Shore area and had been up since the crack of dawn doing these well calculated and kindhearted surprises.

We had rented a van for the day so that we could all travel together but Matt just stuck by Jake and the car rides were uncomfortable and unusually quiet. It was so beautiful in each moment where we made our surprises known to the lucky chosen but I couldn't even feel the magic the way I wanted to with my broken heart and Matt by my side not even looking at me. Linda came to mind again and I could relate to what Linda must be going through but unlike Linda, I couldn't follow Matt around begging him to forgive me. That wasn't my style. I would just give him time to process it all and then force him to talk to me. Today was too important to bring in our personal problems into the important tasks at hand so I just tried to keep my chin up and complete the important missions. Although, my eyes were red from crying and my heart was heavy with sadness, I could act after all, and this was my Oscar performance.

After our morning deliveries, we grabbed lunch together at a diner to refuel and I have never felt so uncomfortable in my life sitting in a booth next to Monica with Matt directly across from me next to Jake. It got to the point where even Jake said something. "*Guys, I don't know what's going on but get over it and enjoy this day. Whatever happened between the two of you, needs to go out the window because we have all worked really hard on this and you are both ruining it for me.*" Jake was right for once. We were ruining everyone's time today. So, I stood up next to the table, taking out $20 to pay my portion of the lunch bill and placed it on the table and said "*you are right Jake. Yes, Alexander Thompson is my father and yes, I didn't tell you guys from the beginning. But this is exactly why. Anyone who knows treats me differently. You can't pick your family but you can pick your friends and I picked all of you. You all are very important to me. Especially you Matt. I am sorry that I wasn't honest but I can't go back in time and change it. I am truly sorry and I did try to tell you first but you were too busy*" I finished and I walked back out to the van and waited there for them to join me wiping away my tears.

Everyone re-joined me in the van and Monica sat next to me and put her arm around me as we drove out of the parking lot and we were on our way to our next destination. We had three more stops this afternoon and the last one would be Billy's big reveal. Billy's event was the biggest and we had advised the media that this was going to be the most important one of all and we had saved the best for last. Media had been speaking about it all day on television and radio guessing who the mystery guest would be. Now more than ever I needed my father to come through for me. This was more than the situation with Matt or about making Billy's dream come true, it could also affect my job if my father didn't show up. Thankfully, the rest of our afternoon went smooth. We made our way to Neptune, NJ to the home of the sister of Jordie. This family knew we were coming because they had already gotten part one of our surprise, the adorable Yorkie puppy. Despite the fact that it reminded me of Matt since we had went to pick him up together in New York City, I couldn't wait to see his little face. The family stood in their door as we entered and Jordie was there too. She introduced the family to us and let us know this was her sister. I hugged Jordie and I could feel her ice melt and the warmth finally coming out. I went over to the little boy in the family to say hello to my friend, as he held the puppy. He let me hold him and I took in his soft puppy kisses and I asked "*What did you name him? I was watching this little guy for a day or two before he came to you in his forever home.*" "*We named him Jordan. Jordan can be a boy name or girl name but Aunt Jordie is our guardian angel so we thought it made the perfect name.*" I answered smiling "*I agree. It's the perfect name for the perfect puppy and he is lucky to have you*" and I gave him one more kiss. Matt came over next to me to see the puppy too and let him kiss him on the nose and then we stood up and the check was presented to the family from their favorite baseball player who couldn't be here in person but sent a video message for them to watch. At least Matt stood next to me and we played with our puppy friend for a bit. Maybe Monica was right and he would come around. I wasn't holding my breath though and my heart was hurting so bad I felt sick.

We were at our last stop before the hospital to see Billy now. The person we were surprising was a Secret Santa himself named Andy. He was a

44-year old man who grew up in poverty in Newark, New Jersey but was now a successful business owner and family man living on the Jersey Shore. Andy had gone into a local Walmart and paid off everyone's balance who had things on layaway for the holiday totaling over $7,000. He did it anonymously but one of the layaway customer's impacted figured out who he was and contacted me. We confirmed with Walmart who reviewed video surveillance that it was indeed Andy who was the Secret "layaway" Santa. After doing some digging on Andy and viewing his social media, we learned that Andy was a huge New York Giants fan too so what better way to surprise him but with a gift of season tickets delivered to his door by a Giants' player. Damion Kipson was waiting in his car service outside Andy's home late that afternoon. We knew Andy was due to be home around 4:15 p.m. and like clockwork, he pulled into his driveway and entered his house. The camera crew quickly exited our van and set up and we stood by them as Damion got out of his waiting car and walked up the stairs of Andy's home and rang his doorbell.

Andy answered the door and being a huge Giants' fan, he immediately recognized Damion and gave him high fives and hugs trying to figure out what he was doing there and barely noticing the camera crew filming his every move. Damion told him about the Secret Celebrity Santa project and why he was identified. Andy was humble as ever explaining that he didn't want the attention but with wanting more kindness in the world, and that he just wanted to set an example and hopefully start a trend. Regardless, Damion was thrilled to present him with his season tickets but it took convincing for Andy to take them. He was really that unselfish. We finally convinced him to keep them explaining that like him, we wanted to do something kind for someone and this was our chance to reward someone causing him to finally cave and keep the tickets. It was nice to not only help needy people but reward people that maybe didn't need monetary help. This was our way of encouraging them to keep on their path of giving back by recognizing the difference they were making in society.

We only had time for a drive-thru dinner after we left Andy's as it was after 5:00 p.m. and there was a lot of prep to be done at the hospital in preparation for our final act. We pulled up to the hospital at around 5:30 p.m. just as Bennie texted me stating that my father was filming still and he was nervous that he wasn't going to make it and would keep me posted. I started to panic. Could he really not push back just this once for me and more importantly for Billy? Monica sensed my fear and asked me what was wrong. "*It's my father. I am not 100% sure if he is going to show up. He always does this to me*" I said crying. "*He will show up*" said Matt as he came out from the backseat uttering his first words to me of the day. "*You guys go in and we will run to get some things for Plan B in case he doesn't and I will text you the details*" shared Monica. We left Matt and Jake with the camera crew at the hospital and we made the van driver take us to a shopping complex nearby and we went to a costume shop and rented a Superman costume as a backup plan. Monica texted Jake and Jake agreed to be Superman if my father didn't show. I was nervous for my job as they were counting on me to deliver the biggest thing they had done as a company and with all this media attention simply stating it was a man in a Superman costume to surprise Billy was not going to go over well for the company, and definitely not for me. Although Billy I am sure would still be happy so I had to at least do something for him.

My job was at risk. I had ruined my relationship with the one man I had ever been in love with, all for my dead-beat father who was going to break my heart even more than it already was by not showing up. More than anything though, I didn't want to let down Billy. Billy had so many struggles and I wanted him to have this moment. I wanted him to feel how special he is and to know we are all fighting this fight with him to get better. I knew he would be happy with Superman coming into his room regardless of who was inside the costume but I knew how much he admired my father. If only my dad could see how much he meant to so many people instead of focusing on how much he meant to himself. I tried to pull myself together during the car ride back to the hospital and Monica helped me re-do my make-up and cheered me up as much as she could.

We arrived back at the hospital at close to 7:00 p.m. and joined the others. We used one of their conference rooms to facilitate the surprise and met with them there to help finish the preparation. We decorated the whole room into a Christmas wonderland and had gifts for other children that were patients there as well as Christmas Cookies and treats for everyone. Media had started to arrive and began set up in the back of the room. The company's CEO, John Fitzgerald, had just arrived too. I had never even met him because he traveled all the time and now the pressure on me was mounting even more. "*You must be Ria. First of all, we are lucky to have you on the team. I heard about the special guest coming today and this is just incredible. Not only is this amazing for Billy but also for our company. I won't forget this*" shared John as he shook my hand. I trembled as he walked away from me and couldn't even answer him from my nerves. My heart was in the pit of my stomach. I whispered to Monica that I was scared he wasn't going to show up. Monica did her best to continue to comfort me. I was trying so hard not to crumble into the floor and I just wished so badly that I could disappear.

At 9:00 p.m. there was still no sign of my father and no texts from Bennie. This was the moment it all was supposed to happen. It was show time so my jitters now officially turned into true fear. We snuck out of the room to delay the guests while Jake put on the Superman Costume and I broke down in tears in front of Matt, Jake and Monica once again. Matt put his hand on my shoulder to comfort me for a brief moment but then left the room leaving me there in tears. Matt walked back down the hall and looked through the window of the conference room standing outside, and just awaited Jake's arrival as Superman. A man walked up and stood next to him. Matt assumed he was with the media and he introduced himself as Bennie and asked if he worked with Alexandria. Matt confirmed and asked "*You are here to see the show*?" "*I actually work with Mr. Thompson. Alexandria is like my daughter. I am so proud of her and I made sure we didn't miss this evening. I know how important this is to her. Growing up, we worked many soup kitchens together, volunteered at multiple hospitals and gave back to the needy. I wouldn't miss this for the world. Giving back has been Alexandria's dream*" responded Bennie. Matt looked at Bennie with confusion on his face and said "*I thought Alexandria grew up with a life of privilege*?" "*Well, of course, she comes from money but that is the farthest thing from how I would describe her. Alexandria has grown into a compassionate woman and is nowhere near what you would think she would be*" answered Bennie. Matt smiled and was angry at himself for judging Ria.

Jake emerged as Superman and entered the room to the children's delight, especially Billy's. Billy pulled at Jake's mask asking if it was really Alexander Thompson inside there and Jake tried to tell him he is simply Superman. The media looked puzzled wondering if this was the hype they had come for – a man dressed as Superman. I could tell another puzzled guest was John Fitzgerald asking me "*where is our guest of honor*?" As I struggled to find the words, in walked in my father carrying an armful of gifts for the kids. My heart melted and tears streamed down my face as Billy ran to my father and hugged him and said "*I knew you would come*!" My father hugged him back and handed out gifts to the kids. And, I could see by the look on John Fitzgerald's face that I had done well. The CEO of the hospital, Lynne, stopped by and pulled me into the hallway as we watched the commotion through the door. I didn't notice Matt leaned up against the hallway wall standing behind us as I chatted with Lynne. Lynne said "*So, I heard an anonymous donor paid off my favorite bone cancer patient's medical expenses?*" I smiled and just responded "*Wonder who did that, Lynne? They must be pretty amazing.*" Lynne squeezed my hand and smiled as she walked away and said "*Merry Christmas Ria.*" I knew my secret was safe with her.

My father took the time to speak to the media and said it was the kindness of his daughter that reminded him what the true spirit of Christmas meant and that he had been so busy working non-stop, and he had let the Christmas magic get lost through the years and he needed this reminder. He said everyone looked up to him but he realized when his daughter moved across the country to take a job where she could give back, that he wasn't the one that should be looked up to. It was people like the ones in this company who were giving back to our community that deserved the recognition, and that he wanted to follow in my footsteps and make a difference. I interrupted his speech and ran to hug him. I knew this moment could easily make my TMZ page but probably never would. It wasn't drama; it was real but I didn't care because this moment belonged to me and my father anyway.

My father stayed till about 10:30 p.m. when the kids were summoned back to their rooms and their families headed out. John approached my father about being more involved in the future and my father happily agreed. I almost felt like I was living a true Scrooge moment as Bennie had his arm around me, and my father looked truly full of joy for giving to someone else for the first time in his life. I had been so caught up in the excitement of my father that when I finally looked around the room as we were cleaning up, I noticed there was no sign of Matt. I guess he was still mad at me but I couldn't understand how else to make him see the real me and I decided that I would try one more time tomorrow to talk to him and if he couldn't see the real me, I would have to let him go. After cleaning up, Monica and the others took the van back to the office to get their cars. I stayed behind and Matt had gone on his own already anyway.

I spent some time having coffee with my father and Bennie before they headed back to New York City at a local café near my office, and then they dropped me off at my car and I headed home. As happy as I was that my father came through for me, my heart still ached for Matt. He had disappeared from the event after my father spoke to the media, and I drove home in silence arriving at my condo at almost midnight with a mixture of sadness and happiness in my heart. This move and this job was not only a physical change but it had been an emotional journey for me too. I wasn't sure what was in store for me now. I felt lost without Matt. I knew my company was thrilled with me but I was too tired to even be happy about that. I went into my condo exhausted and put on pajamas. I tried to calm down my nerves to get myself to be tired enough to go to bed, especially after having a coffee so late into the evening. There was a knock at my door just as I was about to turn off the lights and I could see it was Roger through the peephole. "*Sorry, it's so late but I heard about tonight Ria. Good job!*" said Roger. I replied to him "*Thanks Roger. I am exhausted but we made Billy's night and I couldn't be happier*". Roger said "*And, Matt, what happened with him?* I was too tired to go into the whole story and just told responded "*It's too much to go into Roger but I am going to try to talk to him tomorrow. It was too busy today with all of the Secret Santa stuff.*" Roger added "*Well, before I go, you also have a Secret Santa so I'll leave him to it*" and Roger walked away leaving Matt standing there behind him.

Matt must have been at Roger's condo waiting for me to come home. I looked up to see Matt staring down at me and he pulled me into his chest and hugged me. "*Matt-E*" I whimpered into his chest "*I thought you were mad at me.*" "*The opposite*" Matt whispered to me and I repeated him questioning "*the opposite*?" He replied "*can I come in and talk?*" I shook my head saying yes as Matt grabbed my hand, closed the door behind him, and led me to the sofa to sit down and talk. My heart was in my throat and the knots in my stomach hurt like I was giving birth. I knew my shivers were from fear and not the cold. Matt sat on the sofa and was staring at the rug in silence which scared me even more. I had never seen him like this before. "*Matt you are scaring me. I am so sorry about what happened. I wanted to tell you about my father and I was going to. I am not the person you think I am. You have to believe me*!" I pleaded. Matt put his finger on my lips to stop me from talking and just told me to not say a word. He told me he needed to get something off his chest and just wanted me to listen and not say anything until he was done. I agreed and he stood briefly and he took a blanket from the edge of the sofa and wrapped it around me to keep me warm as he sat back down on the sofa next to me and began. If only he knew I wasn't cold but scared to death.

"*Ria. From the moment I saw you, I knew you were the one for me. When I slept over that night after your dinner with your father and your body was next to mine, it took EVERY ounce of humanity for me to not touch you. I didn't sleep at all that night because I wanted you SO badly. I hung out at Roger's place because I wanted to see you. And, when we kissed in the bar for the first time, kissing you was incredible and it was the best kiss I have ever had in my ENTIRE life. I REALLY mean that. What I am trying to say is that you are <u>everything</u> to me Ria. Your hair, your blue eyes, your body but not just the physical stuff... it's your personality, your heart. It's just you. You are the most beautiful girl inside and out on this entire planet. I know you can have any guy in the world who has so much more than I could offer. When you revealed that Alexander was your father, at first it scared me because I knew you came from a different world than I did. And, when I looked you up and saw the kind of things that were being said about you, I started to doubt you were ever the girl I had fallen for and I got scared. I couldn't comprehend it all and needed* *time to think. I'll admit I was disappointed that you didn't tell me sooner too, although I know you tried to."*

"Last night when I spoke with Bennie, he reminded me of the girl you really are with his kind words. He didn't know anything about me or our relationship so I knew he was telling me from his heart. I ran out of the hospital tonight because I couldn't bear losing you and I was mad at myself because I had judged you just like you thought people would. The truth is, you didn't let me down Ria. I let you down. I realized that my reaction was exactly why you didn't share this fact when you moved here and started working with the team. I am the one who is sorry. And, I know it was you that paid off Owen's medical expenses too. I know you didn't know it was my cousin when you did it either. You couldn't have because his bill was paid off well before I told you but that was probably the single most selfless thing I have ever seen anyone do Ria."

"But regardless of your father, your wealth or what you did for Owen, there is something that I need to tell you because if I don't I will always regret it. Even if you don't feel the same way, I would rather say it and know I tried rather than live with the regret of not telling you." "And that is, Matt paused and looked me in the eyes, *"that I am in love with you Ria. With all my heart. And, not the kind of love that we are dating and spending time together. This is a different kind of love than I have ever felt before. This is the kind of love I have been searching for my entire life where I already know I want to spend the rest of my life with you kind of love. I don't want to freak you out but I would literally marry you tomorrow. I LOVE you so much it hurts! I wanted you to know because if you even remotely don't feel the same way, I would rather know now and try to get over you while I still can because my heart just literally can't take it*" said Matt.

I grabbed Matt's hands and looked him in the eyes.

"*Matt. I knew I loved you from the moment I saw you too, and I didn't even know why. Matt...you are the man of my dreams, inside and out. I can't imagine being with anyone but you. I've never felt this way for anyone in my life and I have zero interest in anyone else. I too love you Matt. I love you more than I ever knew I could love someone. It's going to sound strange but I would marry you tomorrow too. Matt, I don't ever want to lose you but I am also SO scared of you.*"

Matt pulled me closer and asked "*why would you ever be scared of me, Ria? I would NEVER hurt you.*"

In my heart, I knew I could never get over Matt if he cheated on me or let me down the way my father had done through the years. I was scared, plain and simple. "*If you ever let me down or went back to Linda, I don't think I could get over it*" I replied and Matt immediately grabbed me and sternly spoke to me "*I'll* ***never*** *hurt you Ria. You are the girl of my dreams. I want to spend my life with you. I need you to believe me. I love you Ria. Please don't convince yourself into not taking a chance on being with me because of what your father has done in the past or my history with Linda*" he told me and I knew he was right. "*I promise you that I will never let you down Ria. Please believe me. I love you and I am sorry for my reaction to your father. I also can't promise we will never argue but we will always resolve it and that I can promise*" he finished and he hugged me. I looked him in the eyes and told him "*I love you too Matt-E.*" "*I love you and only you, the real you*" responded Matt and then he added "*I want you to be mine.*" I paused to find the words and just asked him – "*Are we going to do this? You and me*?" I smiled at him. "*If you'll accept my poor Ms. Pac Man skills and inability to beat you at Skee-Ball, then damn right we are! God, I love you so much*" said Matt smiling and then he kissed me, lifting me off the couch and in the air before placing me back on the ground, and then just kissing me again for several minutes.

I have never felt such a moment of pure joy hearing how Matt felt about me and knowing for the first time in my life, I felt the same way. This was the happiest moment of my life so far, and his too. I glanced over the fireplace to see the picture of my mom looking at back at me and I smiled as I hugged Matt. She was my Christmas Angel watching over me and I hoped she could look down on me at this moment and smile. I pictured her still on that beach with the sunset behind her and a margarita in her hand smiling because she knew her daughter was loved. I hoped she was at peace and I knew I finally had found mine as I turned back and faced Matt. Matt was the best Secret Santa of the day in my eyes. Matt and I kissed and he lifted me up and carried me to the bedroom. Matt was mine and I was his. My heart felt full for the first time in my entire life.

Chapter 11
ALEXANDER THE GREAT – FATHER

Several months had gone by since Superman had shown up for Billy. The warm air of summer had finally made its way to New York City, my new temporary home for the upcoming few years while I filmed my feature films here. I was tremendously engrossed in my character Adam and making it back to my love, Lily. This film was set to be one of my greatest performances and I couldn't wait for audiences to see it. Even better though is that Veronica and I had slowly started our own love story off camera too. You always hear about on-set romances and how they fall apart but Veronica and I were determined to beat the odds. We had both made mistakes in our lives and in putting our career before everything. We could relate to that in each other and make a change for the better together too. It made us stronger. Veronica had two children that were college aged. She, like me with Alexandria, wasn't around much during their youth having always been on a movie set. But, she was there for the important moments, unlike me. We were both at a point in our lives where we realized what was most important. We weren't kids anymore and we had to make the most out of this amazing life we have. I think Alexandria was just happy that I was actually spending time with a woman that was my age for once. I had been good on set - no meltdowns, no crazy demands. When I did have time off, Veronica and I traveled together. We actually used the swimming pools, the tennis courts and the cars. We were slowly falling in love and for the first time since Carissa, I was committed to someone, and wanted to be. We had finished filming the first movie and had a brief hiatus before we had to start the second installment. These time traveler movies were going to catapult our big careers to an even bigger caliber if that was even possible. Adam and Lily would soon become the next iconic characters for sure.

Alexandria is busy still working at Shore Events. She is totally in love with Matt, and Veronica and I adore Matt too. We have spent a lot of time with them when we aren't filming. I remembered to finally enjoy the simple things in life like Alexandria had always wanted me to. We spent time, along with Bennie, at Alexandria's condo having countless dinners and game nights with Matt and Alexandria. I had also met all of her friends – Monica, Robbie and McKenna, Roger and Jake. Proudly though, I am most honored that I've also gotten more involved to help Alexandria's employer, Shore Events, through starting a scholarship fund for future students who were impacted by drug usage in their family. It was a way that I could honor Carissa. I didn't want her life to have meant nothing because that was the farthest from the truth. Her loss was a tragedy to us all and she did mean something and always would, especially to me and her daughter. She gave me my most precious gift in life, my daughter, Alexandria. This scholarship was also a way for Alexandria to keep her memory alive. It was something we could do together as well to pick recipients each year.

I was all over the news for once but for good reasons. The media had picked up the good things I was doing for once instead of the bad things I had done. This role though was big news too. "The Time Traveler – The Regime" was still in post-production but it was all any one could talk about in the movie business. Veronica and I were having so much fun filming these movies and I myself was anxious to see how they had put it all together and how the first movie in the series would turn out. Everyone kept trying to see if Lily and Adam would end up together in the end or be forced to lose each other to change the future for the better for humankind. Of course, having read the scripts, we knew the answer to that but our lips were sealed. Of course the love affair I was having with Veronica though was an even bigger story and made front page news on every gossip magazine and news column you could think of. Hollywood never really changes does it? Romances in this world always got the most attention, especially for the rich and famous. And, someone at our level of popularity was no exception. We had our own name just like many other celebrity couples before us. We were "Alexica" to combine the Veronica and Alexander names. It was highly ridiculous but it sold magazines I guess.

Alexandria had nothing but good times ahead of her. I should know as Matt was expected any minute to show up at my Penthouse in New York City to talk to me. Veronica and I were staying here to make it easier for filming and he told us he would come by and not to tell my daughter he was here. I think we all knew why. Our place was on Park Avenue overlooking Central Park on the 92nd floor. It was by far one of the most elegant homes in all of Manhattan. The views were amazing and what sold us was the enormous dining room and library. We don't go out in public too much so having as much as we can in a home is important. With six bedrooms, we can have friends stay too very easily. It was much easier to get around Manhattan unnoticed for some reason though versus Los Angeles. And, even if someone recognized you in New York, most of the time they didn't seem to care, or at least that's what they wanted you to think. If you stay out of the real touristy parts of New York, it's surprisingly residential and you do feel like you are in another world living here. The only thing I can't get used to is the noise. It doesn't matter if it is 3:00 p.m. or 3:00 a.m., this place truly never sleeps and neither do taxi cabs and cars honking their horns constantly. But, you get used to it. Veronica is in the kitchen making coffee and Bennie is still sleeping when the doorman tells me that Matt is on his way up.

"*Hey Mr. Thompson*" said Matt shaking my hand and then pulling me in for a hug as he exited our private elevator. "*You said it was important so I am anxious to know what brings you to see me*" I ask but deep down, I already knew what he was here for, and I walked him over into the den. Matt enters into the apartment and nervously takes a seat in the den across from Alexander and continues "*This is the most important question I will ever ask you so I wanted to do it in person. It's about Ria. Alexandria to be exact.*" Matt pauses knowing Ria was not how her dad referred to her. "*You know what your daughter means to me and there isn't a day that goes by that I don't wake up and know how special she is. This girl is not only going to change the world, she has changed my world. What I am trying to say is that I love your daughter more than I never knew I could even love someone. I wanted to come in person to ask you for your permission to ask her to marry me. I have a plan in my mind and want to do it this weekend but it didn't feel right without your permission first.*"

I thought about using my acting skills to make him nervous but I was too happy to go in that direction and just got right into it "*You absolutely have my permission and I couldn't be more thrilled*" and I gave Matt a hug and Veronica came running in with hugs for Matt too as she had been listening the whole time from the kitchen. "*Thank you so much Alexander. I am honored to be a part of your family but just cannot wait to ask her. I am so excited*!" responds Matt. "*Should we go get Bennie?*" I ask Matt and he nods his head and said "*I wouldn't want it any other way without getting his permission too.*" Bennie awakens and we bring him in the room to share the news. Bennie needed to hear it first as well as he was a father figure to Alexandria too. We all knew she wouldn't want it any other way and how much Bennie meant to her. To none of our surprise, Bennie cried like a baby when Matt shared his news. Matt knew he had the approvals he needed, and couldn't be happier.

Matt also filled us in on his plans to surprise Alexandria and how we could help him. Matt looped us in and we made arrangements to make this special moment happen. I would have to have my staff in Los Angeles look through some of my old stuff to find what he needed but we could make it happen. She was going to love his surprise, not only for the proposal but because of how thoughtful it would be. It was going to be an extraordinary moment for Alexandria and I knew none of us has to worry about what her answer would be. We already knew that three-letter-word answer. We also knew that Alexandria had found her life partner in Matt. This move she made to New Jersey wasn't just about her career or her independence, it was more than that. She had been searching to figure out her own sense of purpose and meaning. She didn't want to be in the shadow of the entertainment industry. She found her career. She found her purpose. But, mostly, she found what she was ultimately looking for - she found Matt.

Chapter 12
MATT-E + RIA

Matt moved into my condo about six weeks ago when he could break the lease on his apartment. Waking up to his handsome face every morning has been the single most important thing to me every day. I've never loved anyone the way I loved Matt. And, I knew we were going to be together until we were old and grey. We did purchase one item together for our place and it sat proudly in the loft area that up until now sat empty. It was a Ms. Pac Man machine and despite hours of practice, I am proud to report that Matt still has yet to beat me. We wanted to buy a puppy together too and had started researching breeders to add to our little family that we were excited to create. That was on the list for this summer so that we could get the little friend trained before the weather became cold again. I knew Roger could help watch him or her while we worked so we had a built-in puppy-sitter. We hadn't decided what type of dog yet but we didn't really care because we just were ready for the unconditional love that comes along with any dog.

Work was busy again too. We had just finished several events to honor and surprise specially selected students with full college scholarships awards. I had been also working hard on the Carissa Thompson Foundation Scholarship that my father and I put together sponsored by Shore Events. We had just presented to our very first recipient just last month. The young man that we picked was an honor's student and athlete despite having grown up not only in a drug-ridden area but in a home where drug usage was prevalent. He received a full ride to his school of choice. It was nice to see my mom's legacy continue and to honor her name. It also helped me keep her memories alive and well. The logo for the foundation was a sunset and it was a project close to both my heart and my father's heart as well. I know my mother never wanted this to happen and I hoped this scholarship would help others pursue their dreams and not fall into the same mistakes of those around them when it came to drug usage.

Matt and I had vacation coming up. We were going to go to St. Lucia for a week at the end of July and took another week off too for our puppy purchase so that we could be home as much as possible to get the puppy into a routine and at least somewhat house trained before we had to go back to work. At least we also worked locally and could come home often to check in on him or her and take them for a quick walk too. Living across from the beach, the off-season would be like a playground for our newest family member but during the summer sadly, it was no dogs allowed. When we would return from vacation, we had another event for work as well that we were working on with local restaurants. It was kind of like "restaurant week" but it was focused on the homeless. We would be offering free meals from local restaurants for only the needy. As a part of coming, there would be resources available to help these individuals and their struggles. We had job opportunities, housing and other information and opportunities to help impact their lives for the better and allow them access to resources they may not have even known are available to them. It was going to make such a difference in the lives of so many people struggling with homelessness, and I knew this event in particular had special meaning for Matt given he had grown up in that situation and he has dealt with homelessness many times.

Life was good. I was happy to be constantly making a difference for others. I was also enjoying the Jersey Shore now that warm weather was here. It was so different now that summer was here living at the Jersey Shore. The once barren streets were now bustling with families and parking was scarce. People watching became a "morning coffee on the balcony and watch routine" with all of the commotion on Ocean Avenue. Mostly though, it was just so relaxing to take early morning bike rides to Ocean Grove for breakfast and long walks on the beach shelling with Matt. We loved this little slice of heaven known as Bradley Beach and it became even more meaningful with Matt by my side to enjoy it. We spent our weekends walking across the street to the beach and relaxing in the sun. We could leave and come back to our place for lunch and then go back to the beach or hang out finally on the rooftop lounge chairs with a cocktail. We hit up the Bradley Beach Farmer's Market and other events at the park on Main Street, and spent our money locally at the small shops and the countless restaurants in the area. Matt moving in meant officially starting our lives together. We talked about marriage and children. Thankfully, Linda has finally moved on and had a boyfriend. Linda and Matt had gone back to just being friends and she finally realized too that that's what was always meant to be. Roger loved having Matt down the hall too and we often spent time together and enjoyed each other's company as always. We were already counting down the days to our Monday Night Football hangouts. And, my father and Veronica were often visiting with Benny and we had gotten very competitive with game nights from games like Pictionary, Rummikub and countless others.

This Saturday, we got up early and took bike rides down this time to Avon-by-the-Sea to meet up with Monica, Robbie and McKenna for breakfast overlooking the water at a restaurant set inside a Victorian Era home called "Columns". They had rode their bikes there too since they lived only a few blocks away and none of us had to worry about parking except for where to lock up our bikes. Monica announced during breakfast that she had some news but before she could announce it,

McKenna did it for her. "*I am going to be a big sister*!" she yelled. "*You are pregnant?*" I asked just to make sure and Monica smiled and cried all at the same time while nodding her head. We all gave hugs and congratulations. She didn't know yet if it was a boy or a girl but McKenna of course wanted a sister. Their family was expanding and we told them our family was expanding too soon but instead of two legs, they would have four. McKenna laughed at that and started begging for a puppy of her own too. Robbie thanked me for bringing dogs up as she must ask for one all the time. As we left the restaurant feeling full, we rode together through the streets admiring the homes and dodging beach goers. We had our own official "biker's gang" Matt joked as we rode around the town until we said our goodbyes and headed back to Bradley Beach. Matt and I spent the rest of the morning at the Farmer's market and then came back and made lunch and had Roger over and sat out to eat on the deck overlooking the ocean. I finally felt peace and happiness inside and had certainly found my place as a Jersey Girl.

Matt and I had plans Saturday night to return to the spot where I had first noticed him, *The Asbury*, for movie night. I hadn't been back since my interview with Shore Events that first summer and was waiting patiently for summer to arrive when it would be warm enough for movie nights to return once again. My friend Claire was supposed to come this week too so we would definitely go back next weekend as well when she here spending some time with us. Matt and I were having dinner first at the Stella Marina Bar & Restaurant. It was one of our favorites and located not too far from the hotel. After Roger left, we took showers and got ready for our night out. I wore my favorite sundress and brought a sweater in case it got cool later or was chilly in the restaurant, and then we were on our way. Normally, we would just ride bikes to avoid parking issues but since we were going to dinner and a movie and it was going to be late, we decided to take Matt's truck and valet park it at the hotel.

After parking, we took the two block walk over to Stella Marina. We arrived at dinner and were both starving. Matt ordered us both margaritas to honor my mom which I thought was sweet, and we ordered our food. We toasted to taking it back to where I first saw my future boyfriend and Matt said "here's to finding the right person to walk through this crazy life with" and we took a sip of the margaritas and I licked the salt off my lips. I ordered their Salmon, which was my favorite of their dishes. It was made in white wine with lemon, tomato, pine nuts and currants and served on top of spinach and mashed potatoes. Matt ordered Filet Mignon with grilled asparagus and whipped potatoes. We held hands and talked about the crazy people that passed the window on the boardwalk in Asbury Park and laughed. We discussed Monica and Robbie's news of their pregnancy and how excited we are and debated having a bet on whether it would be a boy or a girl in the office. Matt and I loved to compete with each other for some reason. I told him I thought a girl and he already thought a boy so once again, we were pitted against each other. Matt seemed on edge all day today but not in a bad way. He just seemed anxious to get to movie night but I could relate as I couldn't wait too! I told Matt I still wanted to use this space they had for movie night for an event when we did something that could work there for Shore Events. He agreed but said it has to be the right thing and in the nice weather since it was an outdoor space. Luckily for us, tonight was warm and the sky was clear and the stars were abundant. It was the perfect night for movie night.

After our dinner, Matt and I walked to *The Asbury* holding hands and enjoying the warm evening. It was a beautiful night and Matt told me I looked beautiful too. We arrived at the hotel and Matt had me wait in the lobby and put me in front of one of their lounge pinball machines so he could go to the bathroom. He knew how to make me happy while I waited for him. I focused on my lack of pinball skills while awaiting him to come out of the bathroom and despite eating a giant dinner, couldn't wait for free popcorn in a few minutes.

Matt went into the restroom to call Bennie. "*Bennie, are we ready*?" "*10-4, it's a go*" joked Bennie. Matt hung up the phone and stared in the mirror talking to himself "*this is it*." He was a bundle of nerves but the good kind of nerves. Tonight was the first night of the rest of his life and he couldn't wait to officially make Ria a part of him forever.

Matt finally re-emerged from the restroom. "*Making space for popcorn?*" I joked and Matt nudged me in the side blushing as I finished up my game and we headed to the elevators to the rooftop lounge for the movie. Matt's hands felt sweaty and I asked him if he was not feeling well. He told me he was fine but he was sweaty and just ran to the bathroom so I felt like he might be getting sick but he assured me he was not. I hadn't even checked to see what movie was playing but Matt said "*it's not like we care. Could be the same movie from the summer you saw me there and I think we will be happy*" and I couldn't help but agree. I figured we would probably be here next weekend anyway once Claire arrived to enjoy this place all over once again.

The elevator doors open to the lounge and I am immediately stunned by what I see. White roses are displayed everywhere and pink rose petals beautifully thrown on the floor, my favorite color. In front of the movie screen are two white chairs with pink tied ribbons. I have a stunned look on my face and am speechless for a few minutes almost frozen before I finally ask "*Matt? What is going on? Did you rent this space for just the two of us? What is happening?*" Matt smiled and said "*Yes, this is a private movie for just the two of us. Let's take a seat and you will see the surprise I have for you.*" I smiled with my jaw stuck wide open in shock and kept asking what was going on as I took a seat and my face still looked astonished as I tried to understand what was happening while holding on tightly to Matt's arm and again said "*I am so nervous and I don't even know why. Matt? What is happening?*" "*Just wait*" he said. "*You know I can't take this, right? I need to know*" I laughed but the movie began.

But, it wasn't a movie at all. It was a slide show set to romantic music and the title was "**Matt-E + Ria**" listing the feature cast as Matt McKinney and Alexandria Thompson. Pictures of me appeared on the screen first from baby photos, to when I was a little girl through today. Then, it switched to Matt and did the same showing his baby photos, him as a little boy and then more recent photos as an adult. It transitioned over to photos of us together from when we first met, work events, and then recent pictures from our relationship. Matt must have had to work closely with my father to obtain these photos and tears streamed down my face as I was faced with the reality of what was happening in this very moment. The slide show ended and I didn't even realize that Matt was no longer sitting next to me. He asked me to stand up and he faced me holding my hands in his.

"*Alexandria Marie Thompson otherwise known to me as Ria. You are an angel on earth to me. I am a better man because of having you in my life. I knew I loved you from the moment I saw you, and I told you when we first got together, that I was never going to let you go, and I meant it. Your kindness, your beauty and your heart make you the most special woman in the world. I love you so much and I don't want to go another day without the world knowing that you belong to me and I belong to you. You are my best friend, my partner and the love of my life. I love you so much. Ria, I have a question to ask you.*" Matt gets on one knee and pulls out a box with ring in it and looks me in the eyes. "*Ria, will you marry me*?"

"*YES!!*" I yell with tears spilling down my cheeks as Matt slides the ring on my finger and hugs and kisses me. Confetti starts raining down and I hear champagne popping around us. We are still in an embrace as we look around to see our closest friends and family who had been hiding and watching the whole thing. "*I had a little help to pull this off as you can tell and I thought you would want the most important people here to be a part of it*" said Matt smiling. My father, Veronica and Bennie come over to us to hug us. My closest friend from Los Angeles, Claire, is here as well along with Roger, Monica, Bennie, McKenna, and Matt's mom and brother too. The ring Matt got me was a cushion cut square diamond surrounded by small diamonds and diamonds around the entire band set in rose gold, my favorite. It was perfect! This was the most magical night of my life. Matt pulled off the perfect surprise and the even more picture-perfect proposal. I asked him again "*How did I get so lucky*?" and he said "*Remember, I told you that I am the lucky one. I love you Ria and I can't wait to marry you.*" "*I love you Matt-E*" I said. I have never felt so amazing in my entire life. Mascara streamed down my face and confetti was stuck in my hair but I didn't care. This was the moment I had dreamed about and Matt was the man of my dreams.

In one year, my life had been completely transformed, I found a job I cared about, friendships to last a lifetime, the man of my dreams in Matt, and my relationship with my father was finally the one I had always imagined having. I didn't need to hide from being a Thompson any longer, although I would soon be a McKinney. Life is short and if anyone ever asks me what my advice is on life, I would say, that you should take the time for the little things, never stop following your dreams, always stop and look at the scenery, be kind to other people, and always exude happiness, even if the times are hard. And for right now I will take my own advice and enjoy this moment. It belongs to me and to Matt and the people important to us. I finally accepted the privileged life I had been given and the place I landed because of it. I was so lucky and blessed and deep down, I always knew it but I finally appreciated it. If I could mentor someone and tell them just one thing in life, it would be this:

Drink the champagne, be a Secret Santa, spread kindness, eat the dessert, play the video game, find a job you love and a person that means something to you, and always remember to smile, especially if you have a margarita in your hand while the sun is setting.

Now, the fun begins…planning a wedding. I can already see the tabloids and TMZ on my trail. But, it's o.k. It's who I am. And, I am finally good with it, and with myself.

CPSIA information can be obtained
at www.ICGtesting.com
Printed in the USA
LVHW031500050521
686579LV00004B/601

9 781647 195137